TRION

A story

TRION

A story

C. B. Wilde

The Book Guild Ltd

First published in Great Britain in 2022 by
The Book Guild Ltd
Unit E2 Airfield Business Park,
Harrison Road, Market Harborough,
Leicestershire. LE16 7UL
Tel: 0116 2792299
www.bookguild.co.uk
Email: info@bookguild.co.uk
Twitter: @bookguild

This work is entirely fictitious and bears no resemblance to any persons living or dead.

Typeset in 11pt Adobe Garamond Pro

Printed and bound in the UK by TJ Books LTD, Padstow, Cornwall

ISBN 978 1915352 040

British Library Cataloguing in Publication Data.
A catalogue record for this book is available from the British Library.

For Rene, Carmo and Sofia: 'soft Beulah's night'

'Fear & Hope are – Vision'
William Blake

Chapter One

The Blowing of the Horn

Daybreak: already many of the citizens of Trion were out working – it was harvest time and there was much to be done. Carts sped out of the main gate of the city, turned left and right off the Great Way and bumped along the rough tracks into the fields. They were empty now, but soon they would trundle slowly back with the fruits of another successful harvest.

Trion was renowned for its agriculture; for centuries its citizens had cultivated the fertile plain which lay between the mountains to the north and the less fertile lands stretching south to the ocean. People came from far and near at harvest time to buy fruit, vegetables and grain crops, for the citizens of Trion produced far beyond their own needs.

To most traders this must have seemed like any other busy harvest day in Trion. But an alert observer might have noticed that the guard on the watchtower, rising high above the city walls, seemed unusually vigilant, straining anxiously to see what the sun's first rays might reveal on the horizon.

They might also have caught murmurings of 'trouble brewing in the river valleys to the east'. Even so, no one could have foreseen the calamitous events that were to begin this day, events more terrible than any previously recorded in the history of Trion.

***

Out in the orange groves Zeth was loading a cart with other members of his band. He was gazing, trance-like, between the rows of orange trees back towards the city which stood silhouetted against the pale eastern sky. Was that the watchman signalling to someone below?

"Come on, dreamer," said Zia abruptly, handing him a basket of oranges to load onto the cart. Zia, a tall, slim girl, was the band leader. She resented this job working with the children. She had hoped to be working with the elders now that she had turned fourteen but instead had been given the job of supervising younger children – 'a responsible job', they had told her.

Startled out of his thoughts, Zeth hurried over to the cart where Han, the driver, sat nonchalantly chewing an apple. Han was a stocky, rugged-looking man. He was lame and had been given a job usually reserved for older citizens. "Aye, you'll have no time to stare with that one," he said, laughing. Zeth grinned in return. He could not help liking Zia. Despite her sharp tongue and surly looks, she treated them well enough, and it was largely due to her that they would finish their work well ahead of schedule and earn some extra free time for themselves.

As Zeth returned with the empty basket, Albo, the youngest member of the band, dropped his basket of oranges on the floor and shouted wide-eyed with excitement: "Look!

Look!" Even before Zeth could turn in the direction of Albo's pointing finger, he heard the Great Horn of Trion calling balefully across the fields: one long, rising note. Two men were holding it chest-high on top of the east wall whilst a third blew. The rising sun caught its great bronze rim, sending streams of golden light into the pale sky. Zeth stood transfixed; for him, this was no horn but a brilliant, weeping star, a portent of doom.

Without a word, Han tossed the remains of his apple to the ground, flicked the reins, and drove off as fast as the old horse would take him.

"What is it? What is it?" shouted Albo, clutching the dwarf rabbit he took everywhere with him.

"Drat!" muttered Zia, looking at the scattered oranges and her only means of transporting them speeding back towards the city. "What are we supposed to do now?"

***

Han pulled up the horse and cart outside the pillared entrance to the Council Chamber and scuttled awkwardly up the steps. He had not sought office; indeed, he had wished to avoid it, but no citizen of Trion could refuse to serve without good reason, and he had none, other than a dislike for meetings and 'idle chatter'.

As Han took his seat in the chamber, the porters swung the great bronze doors closed, signalling that all were now present and that the meeting could begin. Thea, Leader of the Council, rapped her staff of office three times on the table and began:

"Citizens of Trion, as you have no doubt guessed from the blowing of the horn, our worst fears have been realised. The Lion-men of the eastern valleys have once again risen up against us. Agon, their new leader, has succeeded in gaining the support of most, if not all, of the tribes to attack our city. Even as I speak, he is gathering his forces on the edge of the Plain of Trion less than fifty leagues from here. Our border scouts, who have been watching his movements for several weeks, report that we cannot safely count on more than two days before he is within reach of the city. After many months of secret negotiations, of going to and fro between the numerous valleys, Agon's preparations have come to a head with alarming rapidity. Even three days ago there seemed no immediate danger. Then, yesterday at dawn, he suddenly appeared on our eastern-most frontier and raised his standard, and like a swarm of bees, his followers came flying out of the valleys to join him."

Thea paused. A stunned silence fell upon the chamber. Zeth's father, Tormon, seated at the furthest end of the council table from Thea, turned ashen. He thought of his child out in the fields, unprotected. What if Agon had sent outriders from his main force? What if even now there were Lion-men prowling around the edge of the city watching, learning, seeking easy prey? He had to grip the edge of his seat to stop himself from leaping involuntarily to his feet and running from the chamber.

Han gritted his teeth and cursed inwardly. Why did he have to be sitting on the council at such a time, a time of hard decisions when even the best course of action may lead to disaster? It would be easier to do as one was told. Even so, he could not prevent himself, at that moment, from voicing an opinion: "I have said this before, but I will urge it upon the council once again," he exclaimed impatiently. "Why do we not send emissaries to this Agon – whoever he is – and ask him what he wants of us? To try to negotiate with him and stop this warmongering before it is too late?"

"Because," replied the councillor opposite him, "it would be of no use. We know what he wants – he wants the Lion-Image back and over that there can be no negotiation."

"Back?" repeated Thea. "Back?! I would urge our fellow councillor to be more careful with his words."

"I beg your pardon, Thea," replied the councillor, "for slipping into *their* way of speaking. I meant, of course, the Image of the Lion which they claim was once theirs but which, as we all know, was wrought by the founder of our great city, Los, and blessed with the power to make our city walls impenetrable to all our enemies."

"Poppycock! Superstitious nonsense!" exclaimed another councillor. "It is nothing but an image, a statue. A beautiful image, yes, but it has no more power than a lump of rock. I say give it to them if they want it so badly and save ourselves a lot of trouble and bloodshed."

"You may be right," replied a calmer, smoother voice, "but is it really the Lion-Image that these savages want? Maybe, but they also want our land – the most fertile and easily cultivable land this side of the mountains. They say the Lion-Image was theirs and this gives them a just cause for war. But what really tempts them is our land and our wealth, and they will never be content until we are destroyed, and they reside upon the Plain of Trion. No, the Lion-Image is a pretext; give it to them and they will find another pretext for war. But our people believe in the power of the Image and whilst we have it, they will fight with confidence. Give it away and you undermine our strength; you weaken the resolve of the people and put fear into their hearts. No, I say whichever of you is right concerning the power of the Image, we must keep it and face the worst."

"I am glad," said Thea, "that we have such a wide range of opinion in this chamber. It is as it should be for it reflects, as this council should, the opinions that are expressed amongst the people of Trion. But please remember, those of you who doubt the power of the Lion-Image, that yours is a minority opinion and a small minority at that. Indeed, not many years ago, such opinions did not exist, or if they did were never uttered. For this reason alone, there can be no question of surrendering the Image to our enemies. We must therefore move on and determine what is to be done in the little time that is left to us."

During this discussion, Zeth's father's eyes had drifted beyond Thea to the stone pillar behind her upon which the Lion-Image stood. What a small thing this was to cause such a fuss! Small enough, indeed, that a child could lift it from its pedestal and run from the room with it. And yet how beautiful it was! Its face exquisitely carved, expressing such calm, fierce power. It was unlike any lion that he had ever seen, and yet like all of them. Its eyes, carved deep within its head, seemed to fathom the very depths of his soul. How could this be? How could a mere carved object seem to possess such life? Tormon found this almost as mysterious as the legendary power of the Lion to protect the city of Trion. Three times the enemies of Trion had laid siege to the city during its long history, and three times they had been repulsed without breaching the city walls. But was this really due to the power of the Lion-Image or to the courage and resourcefulness of the citizens of Trion? And why was this image – a lion – which was meant to protect them, an image also of their enemies, the Lion-men?

These and other questions often perplexed the otherwise tranquil thoughts of Zeth's father as he sat beneath the Lion-Image in council meetings, but he did not pursue them. He was a practical man, a soldier, and he usually thrust them aside as idle speculation. Today, however, it was Thea who broke in upon them: "Our Captain of the Guard seems deep in thought – what is his opinion of these matters?"

For an instant he was startled, but he quickly gathered his wits and spoke: "This is not a time for words but for action. You have told us we have at most two days to prepare for an attack upon this city. Very well then – let us prepare for it. Many times have we rehearsed for such a day, and every citizen of Trion knows what he must do. Let us then organise our people to bring within the city walls every morsel of food that time permits and to destroy that which cannot be harvested. Let them prepare our defences both without and within the city walls. When we have set these actions in motion we may return here and debate these issues at greater length – until then we must prepare for the worst and hope for the best."

A murmur of assent rippled round the Council Chamber; then Thea spoke: "As usual, Tormon, your thoughts are practicality itself. You are right – we must not lose any of the precious time that is left to us. Let us go then from this chamber and set our people upon a war footing. I suggest that we resume our meeting here at noon. Are we all agreed?" There was a murmur of assent. "Then I declare this meeting closed." Thea rapped her staff upon the table; the great bronze doors swung open; and the councillors sped from the chamber – all, that is, except Han, who limped awkwardly behind, cursing under his breath.

Chapter Two

Skirmish on the Plain

Yan scurried down the grass bank, moving in a zigzag line from bush to bush in order not to be seen by the Lion-men below. They were just visible through the breaks in the foliage around the clearing on the edge of the woods.

Yan and his companion, Dava, had been following this troop of Lion-men for several days now, hoping to learn something of value for their fellow citizens back in Trion. Yan and Dava were scouts detailed to ride the outermost reaches of the Plain of Trion and to report to the city any unusual or threatening movements by their restless neighbours to the east.

If only he could get close enough, without being seen, to hear what they were saying, he might be able to take back some vital information. Then he, Yan, would be a hero amongst the citizens of Trion and confirm his reputation as one of their most cunning scouts. He was almost there now, and he could hear their voices rising and falling excitedly.

The troop which they had been following had met up with a larger group of Lion-men from another tribe and now their leaders were sat cross-legged, surrounded by their men, engaged in urgent discussions. A few more paces now and he would be able to make out what they were saying. His heart beat louder and faster as he drew near; one clumsy move or one chance glance in his direction would reveal him, and then it would be a long run back to where Dava was waiting with the horses, keeping them quiet.

He took a deep breath and, with trembling limbs, stepped cautiously towards the edge of the clearing. Almost as his foot touched the ground, as though it had triggered an alarm, a loud whinny and a cry rent the air behind him. Instantly, every figure in the clearing looked in his direction. He froze in panic – surely, they could see him? But no, they were looking beyond him up the bank towards the thicket where Dava was holding the horses. Something must have happened – Dava must have been discovered.

Without thinking, driven only by instinct, Yan shot to his left, keeping low under cover, gambling that the noise of the startled Lion-men leaping to their feet would cover his noise. He made his way back, stooping as he ran, his left hand tilting his sword away from the ground, his right sweeping vegetation out of his path. He ran in a large arc, avoiding the straight line of vision between the Lion-men and the thicket where his only means of escape – his horse – lay. The Lion-men ran out of the clearing, some carrying spears, others drawing swords, but then stopped, summoned back to mount their horses, their leaders worried that they might run into a force greater than their own. Yan, seeing this confusion, prayed that it might save his life.

So terrified was he of the danger behind that he almost forgot the danger that might lie in wait in the thicket. He pulled himself up just in time – there on the ground lay his friend, his sword half drawn in his hand, a spear sunk deep into his chest. One Lion-man was rummaging through his clothes, another through the bags on the horses. Yan stood for a moment transfixed, then, woken from his stupor by the sound of his pursuers now galloping towards the thicket, he hurled himself in a frenzy of rage and fear at the two Lion-men in front of him. The first scarce had time to turn and face his assailant before Yan's sword had whipped across his throat, sending a jet of blood spurting in front of his startled face. Then Yan lunged across the thicket, plunging his sword into the second Lion-man's chest. He fell to his knees uttering two muffled cries, his breath taken away. Frantically, Yan tried to pull his sword out but succeeded only in pulling the Lion-man down onto his face, the sword still buried in his chest. He kicked the man over onto his back; as he did so, a fountain of blood welled up from his mouth and a strange gurgling sound came from his throat. Yan felt sick, but he found the strength to put his foot on his dying enemy's chest and yank the blade out.

Yan rushed for his horse, but then, remembering that Dava's was faster, he mounted that instead. He dug the spurs into the horse's flanks, and with a shriek, it bolted out of the thicket and down the gentle slope towards the Plain of Trion. He had not gone a hundred yards when he noticed a group of seven or eight Lion-men converging on him from the left. They had seen him emerge from the thicket and had left the main body of riders, who had gone there to investigate, to give chase to him. Yan veered to his right and screamed into the horse's ear, "Faster! Faster!" Now it was just a question of speed; if but one of his pursuers had a faster horse than his, he was doomed.

Yan was terrified; he knew the odds were against him, but he hoped against all the odds that his dead friend's horse would be faster than all those behind and would save him.

After a short while, he risked a glance behind. One rider was gaining on him; two were holding their own; the rest were falling back. He felt a surge of utter panic. "Go! Go! Go!" he screamed at the terrified horse sweating between his legs. A few seconds later, the fastest pursuer was now quite close and drawing back his spear. Yan, collecting himself a little, watched carefully, looking back under his arm as he rode. As the Lion-man hurled his spear with a cry, Yan lurched his horse to the left, gritting his teeth and bracing himself. The spear glanced off the side of his right arm, drawing blood. Yan cried out and dug his spurs into the horse which gave an extra brief spurt of speed, whilst the Lion-man on Yan's tail, slowed by the action of throwing, fell back a little.

It was only a brief respite; slowly but surely, he began to gain on Yan again. Now he drew his sword. This time there would be no mistake – he only needed to delay Yan long enough for his friends to catch up.

Yan's mind raced furiously. What could he do? How could he escape? Then he remembered, the river, now less than half a mile away. It was spanned only by a wooden bridge supported by ropes – if he could only make it there then he might… but there was no chance, already the Lion-man's horse was within spitting distance of his and out of the corner of his eye he could see his enemy up in the saddle, his sword raised ready to strike. In desperation, he pulled a small dagger from his belt and flung it behind him. It hit the Lion-man's horse full in the face. With a loud, piercing whiny, the horse reared up, throwing its startled rider from the saddle.

Yan's heart leapt with hope, but he was not out of it yet; there were still two more close enough to catch him if he made even the slightest slip. Now he could see the river winding before him and there, just to his left, the bridge. He urged the horse quickly down the bank. The horse's hooves slithered on the flimsy wooden structure, but it quickly regained its legs, and in a flash, he was across. Now for the ropes. In a frenzy, he hacked away at one of the supports. The first Lion-man thundered onto the bridge. Using both hands now, Yan hacked furiously at the frayed rope which at last gave way. The bridge lurched to one side, sending both Lion-man and horse sliding off into the river. The second rider brought his horse up to the edge of the bridge, now leaning dangerously to the side, and hesitated. Quickly, Yan worked away at the second support until it, too, broke, sending his end of the bridge falling into the river. The last group of Lion-men now drew up, joining their companion on the other side of the river. Yan waved his sword at them defiantly, then turned to begin his long ride back to Trion.

Exhilarated, overjoyed at having escaped, Yan sang and talked excitedly to his horse. But soon, tiredness and the slow dull ache in his wounded arm overcame his high spirits. Back there he had left his friend, dead. He knew his family well and already could feel their grief. Moreover, his mission had been a failure. He had heard nothing and learnt nothing, save the limits of his own courage.

Chapter Three

In the House of Images

It was dusk and, above the city of Trion, the stars began to appear. They shone now as they had shone the night before, before the blowing of the horn and the excitement and panic that had swept the city. They shone as they had shone down the centuries has the people of Trion had cultivated their fields and lived together in peace and harmony. To them nothing had happened, all was still the same, and they continued their eternal march across the sky, remote from the hopes and fears of the citizens of Trion.

Zeth, sitting on the steps to the Council Chamber, looked up at them. He sensed their remoteness and indifference, and they made him feel small and unimportant. He stared at them while his mind drifted over the events of the day. Zia, resourceful as ever, had commandeered a cart from another band, and so they had been able to bring their last load of oranges into the city which was by then buzzing with excitement. Then the bells had rung in every quarter, summoning all citizens to hear emergency directives issued by their councillors. Instead of the free time he had been looking forward to, Zeth found himself out in the fields again, helping other bands to get as much food as possible into the stores. Soldiers on horseback swept out of the main gate in every direction, whilst others began to fortify the city against an attack. All the markets were closed down and foreign merchants advised to return to their homes – no food was to leave Trion now.

Only when the light began to fail did the weary citizens of Trion wander back into the city, exhausted and enervated by the day's events. Then a rider appeared out of the east. He was slumped forward in the saddle; his face was pale and drawn and his right arm hung loosely by his side, covered in congealed blood. As his tired horse cantered slowly up to the city gates, the soldiers on guard there rushed up to meet it and led horse and rider quickly to the Council Chamber. There they helped the rider from the saddle and half carried him into the chamber where the councillors had been sitting since noon.

This event sent waves of excitement through the populace. People began to talk of 'a great battle' in the east. Rumours of heroic victories and terrible defeats swept the city. Children, now released from their duties, fought imaginary battles in the streets so that the clash of wooden swords and cries of 'Die, Lion-man!' could be heard everywhere.

Zeth shied away from these imaginary battles. He could only fight in anger and found this play-fighting irksome. Besides, he was far too worried to play. Why did everyone else seem so happy and excited whilst he was anxious and fearful? Did they not realise that they or their families might die soon? Or were they simply braver than him? Of course, there were the famous walls of Trion which, it was said, would never fall to an enemy. But were they so strong? Did the Lion-Image really have the power to defend them against any foe? And besides, that did not prevent people from getting killed. In all the stories he had heard about the victories of the people of Trion over their enemies, there had always been casualties. There was Igor, who at the end of the last siege of Trion, had led the final charge out of the city gates and swept the last remnants of the Lion-men before him. He was made a great hero of Trion – his statue stood in the market square – but he had died in that last charge.

Then there was Aza who, when there was a surprise attack upon the city, had placed her unit of archers between the attackers and the city gates and poured flight after flight of arrows into them whilst the last remaining citizens got inside the city walls. Aza and all her fellow archers had died before they could beat a retreat into the city. Whilst Zeth marvelled at such heroism, he could not help thinking that if it had been his mother or father, he would have wished that they had been a little less brave and had stayed alive.

Zeth was startled out of his thoughts by a group of boys who had just turned a corner and had noticed him. "Ah! Look – a Lion-man! Let's get him!" shouted one. They ran round him, shouting and making mock thrusts at him with their wooden swords.

"Clear off!" shouted Zeth. "I'm not in the mood."

"You're never in the mood," replied Daan, a large, belligerent boy whom Zeth did not much like.

"And you, the son of the Captain of the Guard! You should be teaching us how to fight!"

"I'll get him," piped up a small voice. It was Albo, who was so small that Zeth had not noticed him amongst the larger boys. He now pushed himself forward, walked slowly up to Zeth and poked him in the stomach with his small sword.

"Albo!" exclaimed Zeth. "What are you doing here? It's getting dark; you should be inside. Besides, you couldn't kill a fly," and with that, Zeth swept Albo's sword aside and prodded him in the chest. Albo staggered backwards and crashed down onto the floor, sending a cloud of dust into the air. At the same time, Albo's dwarf rabbit popped its head out of his pocket and sniffed the air to see what was going on. There was a roar of laughter followed by a shout of, "There you are, you little scoundrel!" It was Zia, who had been looking for Albo for some time.

Since he had been placed into Zia's band, Albo had clung to her as though she were his elder sister. His parents had died in the fever which had swept the city some years earlier. As was the custom in Trion, Albo had been entrusted to the care of his nearest adult relatives, in his case an ageing aunt and uncle. They felt Albo to be something of a burden and tolerated him rather than welcomed him into their home. So, after the band's work was done, Albo would follow Zia around like a lost sheep.

Zia, for her part, made out as though he were a troublesome nuisance whom she reluctantly looked over. But anyone with eyes in their head could see that she cared about Albo and found some comfort herself in the company of her 'little scoundrel'. Zia had troubles of her own. Her father had left Trion whilst she was still young 'to do a spot of trading in the south' and had never returned. For Zia, it was something of a relief – it was said that her father had a terrible temper and would beat both her and her mother when he was drunk, which was all too frequent. Zia and her mother could not get on, and her life at home was miserable. So, she looked after Albo as though he were her own little brother, and they provided for each other a strange sort of companionship.

"Look, men, a ferocious Lion-woman!" shouted Daan, and he made a move as if to cut her in half with his sword. But Zia was also not in the mood, and in a flash, she grabbed his wrist, kicked him behind the knee and sent him sprawling in the dust.

"Clear off, the lot of you!" she shouted, and the boys, making sounds of mock terror, sped off. Nor was their fear entirely affected; Zia had a fierce temper and was known to have got the better of many a lad who had crossed her.

"Come on, you," she said to Albo, taking him by the hand. "Your aunt would kill me if she knew where you were at this hour," and off they went, hand in hand, leaving Zeth alone once more.

Zeth sighed and rose to his feet. Yes, he thought to himself, as the son of the Captain of the Guard, I should be the last boy to be frightened of war. Yet that was partly why he was so frightened – would not his father be one of those most likely to be killed? He walked out of the dusty square and along the hard, smooth cobblestones of one of the main streets of the city leading down the side of the Council Chamber. Already, the torches had been lit upon the chamber walls, sending great flickering shadows across the street as he passed them. The smell of burning oil was somehow comforting to him – at least for the moment, all went on as normal in the city.

At the end of the Council Chamber, the wall continued until it was broken by an archway which opened into a complex of buildings called the Houses of Learning. Zeth walked through the archway and followed the path that wound its way between the numerous houses, which were now lit like lanterns by torches burning within. Each house had its name inscribed on the lintel over its door – 'House of Fire', 'House of Light', 'House of Earth', 'House of Seeds', 'House of Numbers', 'House of Healing' – each name indicating the kind of learning to which the house was dedicated. It was here that the citizens of Trion continually improved their knowledge of agriculture, and of many other things, and it was here that the children of Trion came to learn much of what they needed to know in order to become useful citizens.

To their neighbours it was a matter of great astonishment that the children of Trion should be allowed to wander freely in such places of profound learning, where matters of the utmost importance to the city were decided – which seeds would best survive a frost, which would give the greatest yield, which earths would best suit which crops, which substances would burn longest and brightest – but in Trion it seemed natural that children should assist in the many 'tryals' and observations needed to determine such things and to learn first-hand how to continue the work that the elders had begun. Indeed, it was said that some of the greatest discoveries of Trion were the fruit of the wild imaginings of children, tamed by the patient investigations of their elders.

Zeth walked quickly past all these buildings and headed right to the heart of the Houses of Learning where the oldest, but now least visited, of all the Houses of Learning stood: the House of Images. This was the house which, it was said, Los had built first – even before the walls of the city had been erected – and where he had carved the Lion-Image which now stood in the Council Chamber. The house was now occupied by Fidias, the image-maker, whose skill in image-making could be traced back through the centuries from master to apprentice to Los himself.

As Zeth approached the house, he heard the tap, tap, tap of Fidias's chisel on stone, telling him that the image-maker was still working by torchlight. He entered through the large, oak-panelled door which he carefully closed behind him. As usual, Fidias carried on as if Zeth were not there, bent intently over his work, tap, tap, tapping the chisel delicately through the stone, his large, bald head shining like a moon in the torchlight.

As he stepped back for an instant to survey what he had done, Zeth could see the image which was being revealed by Fidias's chisel. It was a strange creature soaring out of the stone like a comet – thin and tapering at the base, full of energy and anger at the head. It was clearly meant to be a horse, but it was unlike any horse that Zeth had ever seen. Its hind legs, upon which the animal was rearing up, were thin and short, almost merging into its tail, whilst its head was a disproportionately large mass of bulging eyes, muscle and snarling colossal teeth. Even Zeth, who was no lover of horses, could see that the arrangement of muscle and bones in the horse's chest was completely wrong. He sighed and said wearily, "The council will never accept it, you know – it looks nothing like a horse."

"Then how did you know it was one?" replied Fidias.

"Well, you know what I mean – you can tell it's supposed to be a horse, but it looks nothing like a real horse," answered Zeth.

"If you want to see a real horse, go to the stables – there are plenty there! Why should I waste my time trying to copy what any fool can see? This is not a horse but an image of a horse, and the two things are completely different – have you not learnt that by now?!"

Zeth looked again at the image in front of him. Half of him agreed with Fidias – he secretly often found Fidias's images strangely fascinating. Sometimes he even found that the images seemed more real than the things which they were images of. But how could Fidias be right, when Zeth's own parents and almost every citizen he spoke to despised Fidias's images and said that he had corrupted the noble art of image-making founded by Los? For many years now, the council had not accepted any of Fidias's work for a public site within the city. Surely all these worthy people could not be wrong? Yet, looking at the image of the horse, he felt he could see what Fidias was carving, not a horse but all the wild terror of a horse driven by fear to the limits of its endurance. He felt wonder at the sheer physical strength of the horse and pity for its terror, and all this strange mixture of emotions aroused by a mere image. Would others not feel it too? Or would they, if he ever dared to express such thoughts, dismiss him, as they did Fidias, as being more than a little crazy? So instead of agreeing with Fidias that what he had created was far better than a copy of 'what any fool could see', he tried again:

"But couldn't you make something now and again that they liked? Then at least you would prove to everyone that you are as good as the image-makers of old, and they might even try to like your other images."

"I could no more do that than a lion could behave like an ox or an eagle like a sparrow. I cannot make the images they want because I do not see things as they do. I do not have their images in my head so how can I carve them in stone? No, you want me to please the council and your parents so that they will not disapprove of your coming here, so that life will be easier for you and you need not be ashamed of your friendship with the old image-maker. But if you come here, you come here for yourself and not for others – you have to make a choice." Whilst saying this, Fidias continued working; not once did he look at Zeth.

Once more, Zeth felt the old conflict rising within him; he felt his stomach churn with it. Sometimes when he was out playing or working with his friends and all this talk of images seemed remote, he felt like giving up Fidias and training to be a soldier like his father. But whenever he felt deeply disturbed or troubled by thoughts that he dared not utter to anyone else, he found himself hurrying to the house of the image-maker. There, he could speak his thoughts without fear of ridicule or disapproval and relieve his troubled mind in the practice of making images.

After a long pause, Zeth said, "Do you think the Lion-men will attack the city?"

"If things continue as they are now, yes," replied Fidias.

"But isn't there something we can do about it?" demanded Zeth.

"There is nothing that I can do about it," said Fidias.

"Nobody else seems bothered," said Zeth. "They're all running around playing games as though it's a carnival or something."

"And you, how do you feel about it?" asked Fidias. For the first time, Fidias looked up from his work and glanced at Zeth. He knew now why he had come. Zeth hesitated for a moment and then replied:

"I'm frightened."

"Good!" said Fidias. "Fear is vision."

As usual, Fidias had succeeded in surprising Zeth. He had felt able to express his fears to him, but he had not expected him to pronounce them 'good' and as for 'fear is vision' – what on earth did that mean?

"I don't understand," said Zeth. "How can it be good to be terrified when everyone else seems to be walking around perfectly happy?"

"If you think that you are the only one who is frightened, then you have less vision than I thought," said Fidias. "But think about it. Only a fool is not afraid of a charging bull or a raging fire. If you are afraid now when others are not, it is because you see the danger before they do, and that shows you have vision, and you will need plenty of that if you are to become an image-maker."

Zeth felt a certain amount of relief. At least now he did not need to feel bad about his fear, though he would still not reveal it to any of his friends. But it was still there, and in an effort to relieve it, he asked, "Do you believe what they say about the Lion-Image?"

"They say many things about the Lion-Image; what do you mean?"

"That so long as it stays within the city, the walls cannot fall."

"So long as people believe in it, the Image has great power," answered Fidias.

"But can the walls fall?" Zeth persisted.

"Of course they can," said Fidias. "If the enemy is strong enough."

"Then the city could be destroyed, and we could all be killed."

"Of course, that is what wars are all about: destroying and killing. Did you think this one would be any different?"

Zeth now began to feel quite faint with fear. In desperation, he gasped, "But the walls have always held before and our enemies driven away."

"This is true," replied Fidias. "And so it may turn out this time. However, it may also turn out differently. Wars are messy, unpredictable things."

Fidias glanced at Zeth again. His ear had caught the panic in Zeth's voice, and his shrewd eye saw the turmoil in his brain. "Come over here," he said and led Zeth over to a shelf at the side of the room upon which lay a deep pile of parchments. He searched down to the bottom of them and pulled out a few of the oldest, now discoloured and crumbling at the edges. "Look at these," he said.

"What are they?" asked Zeth.

"These are some examples of your best work," he replied. "When you were too young to understand that you were supposed to copy 'real things' and drew only what you, Zeth, saw and not things as everybody sees them."

Zeth looked at the delightful images in front of him, of his father, his mother, of people working in the fields and in the marketplace. They were crude, childish things, but they seemed fresh and alive, and they reminded him painfully of all the things that he loved and that he feared would be destroyed. Why had Fidias kept these all these years? Before he could ask, Fidias had placed a large, clean piece of parchment on top of them and said: "Now, child, work. Show me your worst fears in images as fresh as these. Show them to me, and in doing so, banish them from your mind, at least for a little while."

So, Zeth took the parchment and the charcoal and the coloured pigments which Fidias gave to him and created beautiful and terrifying images out of his pain and fear, and far into the night, the lights flickered in the House of Images long after they had died in all the other Houses of Learning.

Chapter Four

The Face of War

"Zeth, Zeth, wake up. The sun has been up an hour already," said Zeth's mother, Lelka, gently. Zeth stirred slowly then shot upright as the meaning of what he had just heard sank in.

"What?! Oh no! Why didn't you wake me earlier?"

"You needed your sleep. You came home so late last night. We were worried about you."

Zeth sped across the room and plunged his face into the basin of water which had been put out for him. He opened the shutters and looked out onto the street whilst he dried himself. Already, people were scurrying about outside. His mother went through the doorway into the central room of the house which separated Zeth's bedroom from that of his parents. She placed some ground cereal, fruit and milk on the wooden trestle table which stood in the centre of the room. Zeth sat down on a stool by the table and began to eat hurriedly.

"Slow down," said his mother. "You do not have to go out to the fields, so you don't have to be in such a hurry.

Your band will be working in the city today. Your father has arranged for Han and the others to collect you when they know what they are doing."

"Why aren't we out in the fields? Isn't there still food to be brought in?"

"It's too dangerous now; the enemy is too near. What cannot be brought in by midday will be destroyed."

"Destroyed! After all the work it took to grow it."

"I know," said Lelka. "But it can't be helped. We must not leave anything for our enemies to eat when – if – they lay siege to the city. We must make life as difficult for them as we can."

It seemed strange to Zeth, this 'making life as difficult for them as we can'. All his life in Trion he had only witnessed people making life as easy for each other as they could. This table that he sat at had been made for him by skilled carpenters and before then had been grown, hewn and transported to the city by foresters. Other people had cut the stone which made his house, and many, including himself, had helped to plant and harvest the food which he was now eating. Everyone in Trion played their part to sustain life and to make it easier for themselves and others, and now here they were planning to make life difficult for people they did not even know – people who would make life difficult for them or extinguish it altogether. He understood what was happening, but he could not feel at ease with it; it somehow went against his nature. He fell silent and continued to eat, staring vacantly into space with a worried look across his brow.

His mother stepped out of the room into the courtyard, on the far side of which stood a target. She took her bow from its stand and chose an arrow carefully, running her fingers along its length and sighting down it to make sure that it was straight and smooth. Then she placed it on the string and pulled it back under her chin; she held her breath and, with an almost imperceptible movement of her fingers, released the arrow. It hit the target a hand's width from the centre. She frowned. Zeth's late arrival the previous night had heightened her anxieties. She was determined to do all she could to prevent any harm coming to Zeth or Tormon, and this target practice took her mind off her fears. She adjusted the sight on the bow a fraction and went through the whole procedure again. This time, the arrow struck within three finger widths of the centre.

Zeth watched her through the open doorway as he ate. He enjoyed watching his mother's target practice. She went through the whole procedure with a calm, natural ease which soothed him. It was almost like a ritual: the way she placed her body with such care at the right angle to the target, the deep breath as she drew back the bow, her muscles flexing along her bare arms, the moment's complete stillness as she braced herself to lose the arrow and then the release of tension as the string twanged freely and the arrow disappeared, to reappear almost magically in the target. She did it all with such deadly accuracy and precision, yet delicately and gently. *Could she really kill someone if she had to?* he wondered.

She placed a third arrow on the string. This time she did not alter the sight but made a slight adjustment to her aim. She drew back the bow with quiet determination as a voice deep inside of her whispered, "This arrow could save my child's life." Twang! The arrow leapt from her fingers, and there it was, buried deep in the centre of the target. The trace of a smile flickered across her face. She put the bow back in its stand and returned to the room where Zeth was finishing his breakfast.

"I don't suppose I need to ask where you were last night," she said.

"No," he replied.

"Why do you continue to spend so much time with Fidias when you know your father disapproves, especially now when there is so much else to worry about?" she asked.

"Because I need to see him – especially now that there is so much to worry about," replied Zeth. "In any case," he continued, "someone has to go to the House of Images, otherwise the art of image-making will be lost."

"Someone, perhaps, but why does it have to be you? And there are some who say that it is better that the art of image-making be lost than that it continues in the way of Fidias."

"But why does everyone hate Fidias so?" exclaimed Zeth, his voice now rising with anger and anxiety. "Are his images so bad? Are they any different from your rings and jewellery that you spend so much time making?"

Almost unconsciously, Lelka folded her arms on the table, covering her hands and wrists – laden with rings and bracelets – under her elbows. But Zeth did not need to be reminded of what they looked like: strange, twisting forms studded with multicoloured stones, quite different from the jewellery sold by the commercial dealers. For some reason, which he could not quite identify, they reminded Zeth of some of Fidias's stranger creations.

"I am not the city's image-maker," she replied. "What I do I do for my own amusement only; it is not serious work, and it is not made for the eyes of the whole people. In any case, they are nothing like Fidias's work."

Despite what she said, Zeth could see the unease in her eyes and hear it in her voice. He did not believe what she said and did not think that she believed it either. She loved her ring-making. He had seen the same look of wrapped absorption in her eyes as she wrought the tiny, intricate shapes as he had seen in Fidias's as he worked with his chisel, and what could be more serious than that?

"Oh, why do you always have to agree with father and everyone else?" he exclaimed. "Why can't you say what you think for a change?"

"I agree with your father because he is right," she replied angrily. "Why should you think otherwise? Oh, would that Fidias were not the only image-maker left in Trion!"

Zeth did not reply but fell silent as he mused over the hidden rebuke contained in his mother's last remark, for many blamed Fidias for an accident which had killed his fellow apprentices and left him the sole heir to the tradition of image-making. It happened many years ago, before Zeth was born and when Fidias himself was a young man still learning his art. He was then held in great esteem by the people of Trion and was the only apprentice in living memory ever to have his work accepted for a public site within the city.

Fidias had a plan for a great monument which was to be unveiled for the Festival of Spring. It was to be carved in the finest marble such as was only to be found in the hills high above the plain of Trion. Many weeks were spent cutting out the marble from the hillside in accordance with Fidias's instructions, but when it was ready to transport to the city, bad weather set in, putting a stop to the work. The labourers returned to the city, saying that they would not attempt to move such a weight of marble until the rains ceased and the ground had hardened up.

Fidias was furious and roared that his images could not wait until 'the earth had turned to stone' and set off with his fellow apprentices to bring the marble himself. One other volunteer went with them: Han, then a strapping young man who boasted he would hoist the little stone upon his shoulder, carry it back himself and leave the cart for the apprentices to ride home in. If only words were actions! As it was, a terrible accident occurred, leaving all the apprentices, save Fidias, crushed to death beneath the marble and Han with his leg broken and twisted beyond repair.

Fidias returned driving the cart, laden, not with his precious marble but with the bodies of his dear friends and Han, pain-stricken and close to death. In Trion, more bad news awaited him for, as luck would have it, his master had died in his absence. Thus, Fidias entered the House of Images as its only image-maker, though for a while it was only a house of death for him.

No one really knew what had happened up in the hills for neither Fidias nor Han would bring themselves to speak of it. Nor was it this that turned the people against Fidias. For some time afterwards, Fidias's images still found favour in Trion. But gradually, Fidias withdrew into himself – and his images, which had always been strikingly different from those of previous image-makers, became incomprehensible to the people of Trion, objects only of derision and anger. Yet, strangely enough, when others spoke badly of Fidias, Han, who had good cause to curse him, said nothing – never was he heard to utter a bad word against the image-maker. As all of this flashed through Zeth's mind, who should break him out of his reverie but Han himself as he appeared at the open window. "Now then, dreamer," shouted Han, "are you finished dreaming for the day and ready for some work?"

Although Han said this in his usual jocular, good-hearted fashion, Zeth could not help feeling guilty. "I'll be right there," he shouted back and dashed about the room looking for the cloth bag containing his midday meal. Meanwhile, Lelka chatted with Han through the window:

"What are you doing today?" she asked.

"We're helping to clear the ditch in front of the walls," he replied. "It's now so shallow in parts that Agon could roll his siege engines right up to the walls without let or hindrance. It should never have been allowed to get in such a state."

"But I thought children were not to go outside the walls today," she said anxiously.

"Don't worry," Han replied. "They shall be only just outside the walls and close to the main gate, and I shall be with them almost all the time. There are scouts right across the plain now, and we shall be safely inside long before any danger is near."

Feeling Zeth bounce into the back of the cart, Han now flicked the reins and they trundled slowly away. Zeth looked back at his mother, still watching through the window. He felt a pang of remorse. He knew that she loved him and wanted only what was best for him, and he hated to cause her to worry. If only this problem with Fidias could be resolved. If only the threat of war would go away.

Zeth looked round the cart. There was Zia, grinning at his obvious discomfort at being late and having to be picked up. Next to her was Albo, chatting away unconcernedly to his rabbit: "Don't worry, we won't let the Lion-men get you, will we? Stay close to Albo, and he'll take good care of you."

Zia poked him in the ribs with her elbow. "Stupid rabbit!" she said. "He can't understand a word you say."

"Yes you can, can't you?" said Albo.

"He's crazy," said Zia. "We're about to fight a war and he's talking to a rabbit!"

"Give him here; I'll make him squeak back," said a loud, gruff voice, and a large boy emerged from the corner of the cart and moved towards the rabbit – it was Daan.

"Sit down," said Zia, casually pushing him back into his place with her foot. "I'm the leader of this band; only I get to eat the rabbit."

"No!" shouted Albo. He knew it was a joke but even the thought of it upset him.

"Daan!" exclaimed Zeth. "What's he doing here?"

"Teo is sick today," replied Zia. "We had to have a replacement, so Daan's band said they could do without him. I'm not surprised!"

Daan glowered at Zia but had no answer. Next to Zeth in the cart, the last member of the band was Hela, a quiet, sensitive girl, two years younger than Zia and her complete opposite. She stroked the rabbit gently between the ears and smiled reassuringly at Albo.

The cart now passed through the city walls. There were two pairs of gates: one on the outside of the walls made of extremely thick wood strengthened by metal straps and an even thicker pair of doors cast from solid iron on the inside of the wall. Between them the wall itself formed a kind of tunnel with holes in the roof. These holes issued from a chamber within the wall which could only be entered from the top. Zeth looked up at these curious holes as the cart passed between the gates. He had often wondered what possible use they could be – he was soon to find out.

Having passed through the gates, the cart swung left, running parallel, for a short distance, to the ditch which, until recently, had become nothing more than a slight undulation in the plain before the walls. Already it had been partly cleared, and men and women were now strung out in lines down its edge, passing large pails of earth up to carts which were waiting to carry it off. This was the work with which the children were to help, mainly in filling up the pails which, when full, were too heavy for the younger ones to carry. As the carts were filled up, they were driven across the plain to be emptied into the river which flowed out of the mountains and passed close to the city to the north.

It was back-breaking work, and Zeth could not help thinking why it was necessary, if the walls really were impregnable, to protect them with this ditch. As they stopped briefly to eat their midday meal, Zeth ventured to raise this question with one of the soldiers who was working alongside them. He gave Zeth a disapproving look. He knew Zeth's father well and of Zeth well enough. "That sounds like a question from one who spends too much time in the House of Images," he said. "Well, I'll give you an answer," he continued. "These walls are our friends. They have kept out our enemies for hundreds of years. They may be strong friends and able to look after themselves, but they deserve all the help we can give them. Now then, let us have fewer words and more work." He finished speaking and handed Zeth a spade.

All this was said in a most disapproving and scornful manner so that Zeth blushed violently with shame and embarrassment. So great was his confusion that he did not stop to think whether the answer he had been given, stripped of its scorn and disapproval, had been a good one.

Daan had observed all this with glee. He loved to see others being chastised and grinned wickedly at Zeth. Zeth smouldered with anger – at that moment he hated Daan much more than the soldier who had humiliated him.

As they continued working, Daan, in order to gain favour and demonstrate his strength, decided to carry the next full pail of earth a few feet up the ditch to the soldier above instead of waiting for him to come and collect it. The soldier gave him an encouraging smile. When the next pail was full, he pushed it towards Zeth, saying, "Now it's your turn."

Zeth now had a problem. He did not want to be told what to do by Daan, whom he disliked and who, after all, was not the leader of the band. But if he refused, it would look as if he were either idle or unable to carry the pail. He hesitated for a second and stared at Daan, wondering what to say. Zia, who had noticed what was happening, rescued him. "Carry it yourself, you great oaf," she shouted. "I'm the leader of this band, and I'll give the orders." Daan glared at her sullenly, then did as she said; he dared not cross the leader of the band. Zia grinned at Zeth who was not sure whether she intervened out of kindness to him or merely to put Daan in his place.

Just then, a horseman appeared at the top of the ditch. He leant down and spoke urgently to one of the soldiers. He in turn shouted to those below, "Right, everyone, back inside the gates straight away!" That message could have only one meaning, and there was an immediate scramble to get up to the top of the ditch. Those in front dislodged earth and stones which fell on those coming up behind, and there was much cursing and shouts of, "Watch what you're doing!" Albo, being the slowest of his group, got an eye full of dirt and slithered back down into the ditch, cutting his knee on a sharp stone on the way down. He sat at the bottom of the ditch crying, a sorry figure. Daan roared with laughter. Zeth and Hela scurried back down into the ditch and, taking a hand each, hauled Albo back to the top.

Once at the top of the ditch, the panic was over. People looked across the plain and there was no sign of danger as far as the eye could see. They now went at a more leisurely pace back towards the gates. Hela sat Albo down and took from her bag the small package of dressings and healing oils which all the people of Trion habitually carried with them. She carefully cleaned the cut and covered it and then removed the dirt from his eye. She did this with the same quiet care and patience which Zeth had observed earlier in his mother as she fired her arrows into the target.

It was then that Albo noticed that the rabbit was no longer in his pocket. "My rabbit!" he cried, distraught.

"What's up now?" asked Zia.

"My rabbit's gone!" cried Albo.

"He must have come out in the ditch when you fell," said Zia. "He's probably still there." Everyone now went back to look in the ditch, but the rabbit was nowhere to be seen.

"Come on now, you lot," said the soldier who had earlier chastised Zeth. "You've wasted enough time already. Let's have you back inside the gates."

"But I've lost my rabbit," protested Albo.

"You'll lose more than that if you don't get back inside the walls," replied the soldier.

"There he is," shouted Daan. And there he was, at least fifty paces out into the plain, sat up upon his haunches, sniffing the air as though he were searching for something.

"I'll go and get him," said Zia, feigning impatience but relieved.

"No, you won't," said the soldier. "It's much too dangerous. You must go back inside the walls now."

"But there's nothing for miles," protested Zia. "Anyone can see that, and he's only there."

"Nothing that you can see," said the soldier. "And you could be chasing that rabbit all day." As if to underline his point, the rabbit hopped a few paces further away from them. The soldier spread out his arms and ushered them back towards the gates. Zia could see that it was pointless to argue further. She rolled her eyes skywards and sighed to show what she thought of the soldier's decision. Albo wept inconsolably and kept looking back until, at length, unable to bear his crying anymore, Zia whispered something in his ear. He stopped abruptly and exclaimed, "But how?" Zia whispered something else, and Albo seemed somewhat relieved, though still anxious.

Back inside the gates they made their way, like everyone else, up the nearest steps to the top of the wall to see if they could discover why they had been brought back inside. The walls were crowded with people all searching the horizon anxiously for any sign of Agon's army. But there was nothing to be seen. Some hailed up to the watchtower, shouting, "What's happening? Can you see anything?" The guard merely shook his head and shrugged his shoulders. Occasionally, a single rider would appear, but always it was one of their own scouts, who, on entering the gates, would ride immediately to the Council Chamber, refusing to answer any questions. After the last of these riders entered the city, both the inner and outer gates were closed. A hushed silence fell on the crowds.

Trion was now completely sealed off from the outside world. All the smaller exits from the city, which were no more than narrow apertures in the walls, had been sealed two days earlier. Zeth suddenly felt himself to be a prisoner. He looked out at the fields which he had worked and wondered how long it would be before he could walk freely through them again. No doubt others had similar thoughts, for there was an atmosphere of melancholy and even, for the first time, fear in the air.

It was then that Zeth noticed that Zia and Albo were no longer with them. He thought nothing of it. Zia was always one for going her own way, and Albo would undoubtedly follow her.

From within the city came the noise of marching feet, distant at first but growing increasingly louder. People now turned round, looking away from the plain and into the city to see what was happening. A large body of soldiers soon appeared, marching towards the gate. Zeth recognised his father leading them. Tormon bellowed an order: "Clear the walls!" Quickly, people began to descend the steps from the walls whilst the soldiers mounted the steps either side of the gate. Soon the walls were bristling with shining armour, shields and spears. The crowds, their curiosity still not sated, flocked into the tallest buildings, some of which were higher than the walls, and emerged on balconies, leaning out of windows and over parapets on flat roofs. Zeth, carried along by the crowd, found himself on the roof of one of the tallest buildings from where he had an eagle's eye view over the walls of the plain below.

Everybody waited expectantly, for what they were not sure, but they were not to be disappointed. After a few minutes, a thin black line appeared on the horizon. Gradually, it grew thicker until it was no longer a line but quite clearly an army of horsemen stretched out right across the plain. As they grew nearer, one could see, in the centre of this host, a number of banners around a denser group of riders, no doubt indicating Agon's entourage. As Zeth surveyed this vast host, his heart felt frozen with fear. But the fear was not just his – it was all around him in the faces and rigid bodies of the crowd. His eye fell on the soldiers of Trion standing defiantly, shining on the walls. A small ripple of relief ran through him, thinly masking the fear for a moment.

Suddenly, a voice called out, "Look! Look!" People looked about, confused, not knowing where they should be looking. Then more voices joined the chorus and hands could be seen pointing at something between the approaching army and the walls.

At last, Zeth saw what they were looking at: two figures running towards the gate, one very small, the other taller, but both unmistakably children. *It couldn't be…* he thought. *No, they were inside when the gates were closed.*

A small group of riders now detached itself from the approaching army and galloped towards the two figures. A moan of dismay went up from the crowd – they would never make it and, if they could, dare they open the gates? "Archers! Archers!" shouted someone. "Where are the archers?"

As if in answer, a band of archers ran towards the gates. "Open the gates!" ordered their leader. The soldiers by the wheels that controlled the gates hesitated.

"Open them!" shouted Tormon from the walls. "One stride's width only."

The wheels spun; the gates swung open upon their massive hinges; and the band of archers ran out and formed a line in front of them. "Arrows!" shouted their leader. The arrows clicked in unison as they were brought to the side of the bows.

"Maximum range," she called. The archers leant back perfectly together, like a line of well-rehearsed dancers. "Loose!" There was a rush of air as the arrows leapt skywards like a flock of birds. They flew in a perfect arc, landing in the earth well short of their targets. The horsemen slowed – they saw the arrows fall between them and their prey and knew that the next time they fired they could be in range. Nevertheless, they continued until the next flight of arrows fell, this time only just in front of them.

Zeth could now see the two children clearly, but he could not believe what he saw – it was Zia and Albo. But how had they got out?

The horsemen now pulled up. They too could now see that they had only been chasing a couple of children and probably considered that they were not worth the risk. But they stayed defiantly just out of range, threatening, menacing. One of them carried a bow himself, and perhaps as a gesture, as a futile act of defiance, he fitted an arrow to the string and loosed it almost carelessly in the general direction of the archers. The arrow soared into the sky where, at its maximum height, it hovered ominously in the wind. Then, like a bird of prey, it fell, almost vertically, earthwards and plunged its barb, with a dull flesh-metal thud, deep into Albo's' back.

There was a moment's awful silence, as when an angel's wings cease beating. Then a low, sad moan of grief and disbelief issued from the crowd. Albo tumbled over, lifeless, like a puppet whose strings had been cut. Zia, whose hand he still held, tried to pull him to his feet, thinking he had just stumbled. Then she saw the arrow. For an instant she froze, her face expressionless, too shocked to reveal anything. In that instant she almost gave up, almost allowed herself to give way to despair. But there was a chance that Albo was still alive, and in pursuit of that glimmer of hope she dug deep within herself and found enough strength to hoist Albo onto her shoulder and run towards the archers, who were now rushing towards her, some firing arrows in outrage at the horsemen, others throwing down their bows to help Zia into the city.

Zeth watched, horrified. He felt as though a terrifying nightmare, which had hovered around him for days, was now becoming a reality. He saw the horsemen turn and ride back towards the army of Lion-men which now stood still, watching across the plain. The man who had fired the arrow was the last to go. He lingered a little and watched, whether in remorse or triumph, Zeth could not tell.

They carried Albo's body to the House of Healing. After a quick look, the healers shook their heads – Albo was dead. In a sense, Zia too died that day. With the death of her 'little scoundrel', something inside of her snapped. As for the citizens of Trion, they too had changed – they had stared into the face of war and had not seen any reason to rejoice.

Chapter Five

Of Arrows and Images

It should have been easy to discover how it was that Zia and Albo had come to be outside the walls after the gates had been closed – after all, one only had to ask Zia. However, Zia would not or could not speak. She stared vacantly into space and said nothing despite the barrage of questions which were hurled at her.

At first, people became impatient with her, thinking that she was afraid to admit what she had done and the tragedy it had caused. It soon became clear, however, that there was something terribly wrong with her. After Albo had been declared dead, she had opened her mouth as if to cry but no sound came, nor did any tear fall from her eye. All thoughts and feelings seemed to be locked inside her head, as if behind walls as impenetrable as the walls of Trion.

The healers examined her carefully and declared that they had seen few cases like this before and that they did not know how long it would be, if ever, before she would speak again. Zia was kept in the House of Healing where she sat or lay motionless both day and night, eating little and only when forced. Her mother and her friends were encouraged to visit her often and to talk to her, offering her words of comfort and striving to draw her out of the darkness into which her poor tortured spirit had withdrawn.

Meanwhile, the soldiers at the gates were carefully questioned, but they swore that no one could have slipped past them after the word had been given that no one was to leave the city. Zeth said that he had seen Zia and Albo inside after the gates had been closed. A careful search was made to see if they had left any sign of how they had got over the walls and out of the city, but nothing was found. For the time being it was a mystery whose secret lay locked in Zia's head, and there it was to remain for a long time to come. As for the rabbit, it was found tucked inside Albo's tunic. Zeth agreed to take it home, where he lodged it in a hutch in the courtyard – a constant, painful reminder of Albo's fate.

After the initial skirmish at the gates, the citizens of Trion braced themselves for an immediate attack upon the city, but they were wrong. Agon knew, like any experienced commander, that it would be madness to attack well-defended walls with unprotected foot soldiers and horsemen. The attackers would be shot down in large numbers whilst only inflicting small losses on the defenders. No, Agon had come prepared for a long siege and started to set up camp. Gradually, around the walled city of Trion, another city began to grow, a city of tents, ramshackle barricades, corrals for horses and a forest of fluttering banners and flags. Strangely, this gave the Plain of Trion a festive air as though a great fair were about to take place.

But soon, more menacing structures began to arise within Agon's camp. Carts arrived daily bearing wood felled on the edge of the Plain of Trion, and from this wood, Agon's skilled carpenters began to build the engines of war: siege towers, battering rams and catapults. Only when these machines were completed would Agon risk a full-scale assault upon the city. Meanwhile, he did not allow the besieged citizens to rest completely. From time to time, groups of mounted Lion-men would ride close to the city, loose their arrows over the walls and then sweep out of range. Occasionally, they would succeed in wounding or killing an unlucky citizen inside the walls, and occasionally the defenders would succeed in hitting one of the Lion-men as they raced away. But this was not the real battle, and everybody knew it.

As the weeks went by, the besieged citizens became increasingly bored and restless. This was something which had not occurred to them, that war, far from being exciting, could be simply boring and inconvenient. They could not go out and work the land; they could not bathe in the river; the children could not play in the fields; all trade had stopped. They did not dare, even, go too far from the centre of the city lest they were struck down by stray arrows fired over the walls. In short, the walls, which they had always thought were the guardians of their freedom and security, came to seem like the walls of a prison. Underlying this tedium was the constant fear of what lay ahead exacerbated by the noise, wafted on the wind, of Agon's men building their engines of destruction. So, they waited, like condemned men, listening to the sound of their own gallows being erected, hovering between boredom and fear.

During these first weeks of the siege, Zeth spent much of his time in the Houses of Learning. He found it comforting to lose himself in the study of numbers, and he was fascinated by the movement of the fixed and wandering stars across the sky. Besides, what else could he do now that there was no work in the fields, no swimming in the river, no chance to wander in the countryside around Trion?

He did not go to the House of Images for a while. After witnessing the death of Albo, he felt, for the first time, a great deal of hatred and anger towards the Lion-men. Why had they come here? What right had they to disrupt their peaceful, industrious lives? And why, above all, had they killed Albo, who could do them no harm? Like most of his fellow citizens, Zeth had come to think of the Lion-men as evil, subhuman beings, not really like them at all. These feelings he knew Fidias would not share or sympathise with. Besides, he felt the need to remain close to his parents and began to grow increasingly respectful of his father's soldierly, practical attitudes. After all, what else could save them from the Lion-men? If all were like Fidias, would not the city already have been laid to waste?

Much to his father's delight, Zeth practised swordsmanship with him in the evenings. Zeth had not shown much interest in such warlike pursuits before, but he was naturally gifted in them, being light on his feet and quick to learn. Tormon even taught him how to throw a real spear and was astonished at his son's progress. Perhaps his dreamer would make a soldier after all? As for Zeth, he enjoyed this time with his father who was a good teacher, being patient and methodical. So, the siege, which threatened to separate father and son forever had, for the moment, brought them closer together and strengthened the bond between them.

But it was not long before Zeth found himself treading the path to the image-maker's house again. It happened late one afternoon after he had been to visit Zia. Several weeks had passed since that terrible day when the Lion-men had arrived, and she was still in a trance-like state, speaking to no one. Zeth had visited her almost every day since. It was not an easy thing to do, talking to somebody who never uttered a word or even acknowledged your presence, and every time Zeth saw her, it brought back to him that terrible event and kept it fresh in his mind, tormenting him. Yet he felt he must visit her and do all he could to coax her back to life again. Zia seemed paler and thinner than ever, and Zeth feared that if something were not done soon, she too would die. Almost out of desperation, he went to speak to Fidias. Why, he could not say. As a pretext for his visit, Zeth took with him some work he had done in the House of Numbers, which he was very proud of and which he was sure would interest Fidias.

When he entered the House of Images, Fidias was sat in his chair staring at a piece of paper marked by a few bold strokes of charcoal, outlining some as yet indecipherable object. He was completely absorbed in thought, and Zeth was convinced that he had not even heard him enter. He had seen Fidias like this before when he was beginning some new project. He usually began by making a great number of these strange drawings, some of which he tore up and threw away as soon as they were done, but others he pondered over, sometimes for hours, making almost imperceptible changes until he was satisfied. At some point, he would lay his drawings aside and, in a great burst of energy, attack a piece of stone or marble with his chisel and labour ceaselessly until his work was done without ever referring to his drawings again.

Zeth had always been mystified by this process. He thought of the drawings as plans, rather like the plans the builders worked from when they were constructing a new house. But unlike Fidias, builders were constantly referring to their plans to check details and measurements. What was the point in making such drawings with so much care and in so much detail if you were never going to use them again? When Zeth had questioned Fidias about this, he had merely replied that it was not the drawings which were important but making the drawings and that, in any case, it was no use asking him since he did not understand it any more than Zeth. Some things, he said, could not be taught; they simply had to be learnt.

Zeth looked at Fidias in amazement. How could he be so completely absorbed in creating new images whilst the city was besieged? "Look," announced Zeth and placed in front of Fidias the pieces of parchment he had brought with him from the House of Numbers.

"Ah!" exclaimed Fidias, startled out of his thoughts. "So you have returned at last. I thought you had abandoned image-making for good. But what is this I see you have brought? Strange images indeed – stranger, some might say, than the images of Fidias. I see you have not been idle."

"I drew these in the House of Numbers freehand," explained Zeth. "Hypasia said that only someone trained in the art of image-making could have executed them so perfectly without the aid of lined parchment and that perhaps Fidias had his uses after all."

"Did she?!" exclaimed Fidias. "Praise indeed – Hypasia is the best mathematician Trion has ever had, and no doubt you are now going to explain to this poor, foolish old image-maker – who no doubt has his uses – what they are."

"Yes!" enthused Zeth. "Each of these lines shows the path of an arrow through the air. It does not matter at what angle you fire the arrow, its course will always make the same shape, and this shape is called a—"

"Arrow? What arrow? I see no arrow," interrupted Fidias.

"Well, no," replied Zeth. "This is not an arrow but the course of an arrow's flight through the air."

"Ah, I see," said Fidias. "This is the flight of an arrow stripped of the arrow itself, of its shape, its size, its colour, reduced in fact to this thin grey line which you have drawn."

"Exactly!" said Zeth, relieved.

"Poor arrow!" said Fidias. "But tell me, why was it fired?"

"Why?" repeated Zeth, utterly bewildered. "But it does not matter why; that is not relevant. This is not a particular arrow fired for a specific reason; it is the course of any arrow fired for any reason or in fact," – and here Zeth's voice rose with excitement as he thought he had latched onto what would explain things perfectly – "it may not be an arrow at all! It could be any missile – a spear thrown through the air or a stone from a catapult – anything, anything at all."

"I see," said Fidias. "This is a line showing anything and everything flying through the air: arrows, spears, stones, failed pastry hurled by angry cooks, chickens kicked skywards by bad-tempered farmers, sandals, rotten fruit or anything else that is to hand hurtling towards mischievous children who have tried their parents' patience too long. Yes, I understand – it is an abstraction."

"A what?" asked Zeth, laughing.

"An abstraction," repeated Fidias. "We image-makers use them all the time. An abstraction is one part of a thing separated from all the rest. Your shape – what do you call it? The course of an arrow?"

"A parabola," said Zeth.

"Yes, a parabola," repeated Fidias. "Well it's just the flight of the arrow without its shape or colour or weight or anything else. In fact, as you said, it could be the flight of anything thrown through the air. Just as these," said Fidias, pointing to the drawings he had just been working on, "are just one aspect, one part of an image I hold in my mind, a few lines abstracted from all the rest. And this too," and here he unrolled a huge canvas lying on the floor under a shelf, "what do you think this is?"

Zeth looked at it, feeling more than a little confused. It was a painting he had seen before which Fidias had finished in the spring. It consisted only of a mass of colour, predominantly yellow, pale at the edges, growing darker and darker towards the centre until the yellow changed into a deep, glowing orange. The colours were intoxicating, dazzlingly bright. As Zeth looked at it, he felt a momentary sense of wonder as he was drawn from the sun-drenched edge of the picture to its deep, dark centre. Then the question that the council had asked sprang into his mind: "What is it?" Fidias had told them that it was a colour of a spring flower. The councillors, some almost unable to contain their laughter, had asked where the rest of the flower was. Fidias, too proud to explain, had rolled up his canvas and stormed out of the Council Chamber to continue his work.

"I don't know what it is," replied Zeth.

"It's the colour of a flower," said Fidias. "A flower stripped of everything else except colour, just as your line is the flight of an arrow stripped of everything except the course of its flight. It is an abstract just like your parabola. But does not your thin line impoverish the arrow? And does not my image glorify the flower? Does it not ask you to look at it as though for the first time with new eyes? Does it not, by showing only the colour, say, 'This is my colour, look at me!'? But this is more than the colour of a flower – just as your parabola is more than the flight of an arrow. For has not the flower drawn into its dark centre the light and energy of the Sun itself, the source of all life? And does not this image reflect this? In showing you the colour of a flower, have I not given you an image of life, of the world? But no!

To see that, you need imagination, something that no longer dwells amongst the people of Trion."

"But no one could know simply by looking that this was a flower," objected Zeth.

"Of course not," replied Fidias. "Nor need they. Nor could anyone know that your line was an arrow in flight. Yet has this ever been an objection against the study of motion or of numbers? No! Show them an image they do not immediately understand, and they deride it, yet show them a parabola or a string of numbers that they do not understand, and they stand with gaping mouths like asses and mumble, 'Isn't it clever,' though they understand nothing!"

"But people know that the study of numbers and motion is useful," argued Zeth. "They know that through the study of flight, our catapults and our archers are better than those of our enemies. And though they do not understand the motions of the wandering and fixed stars, they know when it is best to sow and best to harvest our crops. Is not this why Trion has been the richest and happiest of places, the envy of all the peoples around?"

Fidias looked at Zeth and sighed. The boy was certainly clever; there was no doubting that. How he found the right arguments so quickly and expressed them so well! But more astonishing was the fact that Zeth was voicing the opinions of others better than they could express them themselves. Zeth himself did not know what to believe – he was torn between the practicality of his father and others, and the power and beauty he felt in Fidias's images.

"Useful!" exclaimed Fidias. "And my images are useless, eh? And tell me, what is the use of laughter and of wonder? And what is the use of filling your stomach and killing your enemies if at the end of the day you are dead inside, if your eyes are blind to beauty and your heart closed to joy?

Beware of those who are only interested in things that are useful; they can never be more than comfortable corpses. We are becoming a people of narrow vision interested only in comfort and security. We grow food far beyond our needs and sell it to those who can grow their own whilst all around there are people who every year see their children die for the want of a little bread. Can we wonder if they now rattle at our gates in hatred and anger? Meanwhile, we hide behind our walls like frightened rabbits knowing nothing about our enemies."

"But do you mean that the Lion-men do not have enough food, that their children starve?" asked Zeth, astonished.

"Of course! Little of their land is tillable; often the valleys flood and drown what crops they can grow. Many years ago, before the Wars, they relied upon us to supply them with food – we traded with them freely."

"But I have never heard this before," said Zeth. "How do you know?"

"How do you know?! What a wonderful question! You ask it of me now only because I have said something that surprises you. What a pity it is not asked of all those things that people think they are so sure of! Promise me that you will ask this question more often, and especially of those things that people never question. When people say that our enemies are wicked, that they are stupid, that they are uncivilised, ask them, 'How do you know?' If they tell you that we have never traded with those who are now our enemies, ask them, 'How do you know?' Listen carefully to the answer, mind, and consider if it does not come down to this: 'Everybody knows that!' or 'I know because I know.'."

"But how do you know?" repeated Zeth.

"Good, good," said Fidias, laughing. "Yes, you must also be persistent, for there are those who will avoid the question altogether. But I will answer your question. I know because I am curious and because I ask questions. I ask them of the traders that come here; I travel, usually during the spring when I need a rest from image-making, and when I travel, I use my ears and my eyes and learn much that the people of Trion never even think about. Admit it, it had never occurred to you to consider whether the Lion-men had enough food or not. Do you know if they make images? If they sing or dance? How they govern themselves? No, because you have been taught to think of them only in a certain way, as 'not us', as wicked, as a threat – was there any more you needed to know? Even the name that we have given them – Lion-men – stops you thinking about them as people. For does it not imply that they are savage, only half human? If I know more about them, it is only because I asked the questions, because I was curious. But why should you believe me? I might be making all this up. Find out for yourself. But be careful to check the information you are given and to always ask those who have something to tell you, 'How do you know?'."

Zeth remained quiet for a while. He was confused, disturbed, excited by the things that Fidias had suggested to him. There were so many questions crowding into his mind that he did not know what to ask or say. He walked over to the window and looked out. The sun was low in the sky, casting long shadows around the Houses of Learning. He noticed the House of Healing bathed in the soft orange glow of the setting sun, transforming its walls from stone to gold. *Could he*, he mused, *'abstract' this colour from the building and yet, at the same time, convey the idea of healing?* He then remembered why he had come in the first place: Zia. Nothing Fidias had said could help her. "But I know that the Lion-men are savages," he said suddenly, almost spitefully, "because I saw them with my own eyes kill my friend who could not hurt them. Now Zia is dying too because of them."

Fidias strode over to Zeth and placed his hand on his shoulder. "I am sorry about your friend," he said. "No one knows better than I how painful it is to lose one's friends needlessly. No one can excuse what happened, but in war all peoples are savages – you will find that out soon enough. But tell me, what ails Zia?"

"She has not spoken since Albo was killed. She will not eat unless forced. She does nothing but stare. She grows thinner and paler daily. I think that soon she will die unless someone finds a way to help her."

"I am not a healer but an image-maker," said Fidias. "But this I do know. No creature will live if it has lost its will for living. Albo must have meant more to her than anyone imagined. If you want to help her, you must find a way to put some purpose back into her life – you must give her a reason for living."

"But how?" asked Zeth. "How can I give her a reason for living?"

"I cannot answer that," replied Fidias. "She is your friend, not mine. You must find a way, not I. But do not concern yourself unduly – I think you may have more time than you imagine. Zia, I know, is a hardy plant, and such plants take a long time to die, even when the roots have been severed."

"And meanwhile, what do I do?" asked Zeth.

"You are doing all you can," replied Fidias. "You are caring and thinking. Reason may not provide you with an answer, but perhaps imagination can, and if imagination provides the answer, no one can say from where it will come or what form it will take. You can only wait and hope. But come, we have talked long enough, it is time to let the imagination do its work. Make me a picture before you go – something with a bit more flesh on it than these parabolas!"

So they worked, the two of them, through the late afternoon and through the dusk whilst the House of Healing turned from gold to purple and beyond the dusk into the evening when all turned to black and the flickering lights of lanterns. And as they worked, they talked about many things: about how Los had built the Houses of Learning but, according to Fidias, had not built the walls, despite what people believed; about what was good in Trion and worth preserving and what should be changed or allowed to wither away; about the Lion-men and their ways, and though Fidias did not know much about these things yet, it was much more than Zeth had ever heard.

At last, Zeth had finished and said that he must go – he did not wish to cause his parents undue concern. He had painted an arrow, showing the whole course of its flight – a perfect parabola. But this was a whole arrow with feathers and an evil pointed head. At its source there was no archer, no reason for its flight, but at its goal there was death and misery. As he left, Fidias rolled up the canvas and tossed it to him, saying, "Keep it. It is good, but remember it is true only in a vacuum."

"A what?" asked Zeth.

"In a vacuum," repeated Fidias. "A place empty of everything, including air. In the real world, things can be quite different – nothing travels along a perfect parabola, and arrows don't always hit their intended target."

He smiled, and Zeth left knowing that, for much of the time, Fidias had been playing with him. He did not have an answer to his most urgent question – how to help Zia – but he had a strange feeling that perhaps he had the beginnings of one. Somewhere within himself, he felt the germ of an idea beginning to grow. He could not see it clearly, but he sensed there was a connection between some of the many thoughts that were whirling around in his mind: Zia's illness, her mysterious exit from the city, the Lion-men, a reason for living. He did not realise that when this idea crystallised, it would determine his destiny and that of all the children of Trion.

Chapter Six

Terror at the Gates

Yan stood on the east wall, close to the gates, looking out across the plain. His arm was healed, but it still ached occasionally, especially when the weather turned cold. He rubbed it now as he paced the wall in a cool, northerly wind. There was, of course, no need for scouts now that they were all bottled up inside the city, so he had been attached to one of the patrols whose job it was to keep a constant watch on what Agon's army was doing.

It had been a boring occupation at first, walking along the same stretch of wall day after day, staring out across the plain with nothing to see but the gradual growth of Agon's machines. But recently there had been more activity and more danger. It was clear that many of Agon's machines were nearing completion, and there had been a series of daring attacks against the city walls during which the Lion-men emptied huge cartloads of earth and stones into the ditch. The attacks were usually begun by men on horseback sweeping in and out of range of the walls. Then several carts would be pushed furiously across the plain, surrounded by a mass of Lion-men bearing shields. As the carts came within range, there was a rapid exchange of arrows and spears until the carts' contents were tipped into the ditch. Then, at an even greater pace, the carts were pulled back across the plain, leaving a few dead and wounded bodies in their wake.

These events were marked by acts of great courage as Lion-men risked their own lives to help their wounded comrades, under fire, away from the walls. Often some were beyond help, having fallen into the ditch or, being left for dead, revived later and found themselves too gravely wounded to move. Their mournful cries floated across the city, giving it an eerie, haunted air, as though possessed by the spirits of the not-quite dead.

From the highest buildings, the citizens of Trion watched these attacks as they had watched the shooting of Albo on that fateful first day of the siege. The atmosphere was almost like that of a sporting event: people cheered when a Lion-man fell and groaned when, occasionally, one of their own citizens was hit. Then there would be a flurry of questions: "Who is hit?" "Do you know her?" "Is he badly hurt?" As in all sieges the defenders' losses were, in these early stages, extremely light and those of the attackers relatively heavy. At first, therefore, people were happy with the way things were going and expected the Lion-men to give up and go before long. But as, gradually, the ditch began to fill up in various places, marking the points where the main attacks would come, they began to grow more fearful and watched these events more quietly, taking little joy in the daily slaying of a few of their enemies.

Yan and his companions stood now at one of the points in the wall where the ditch was being filled in – it would not be long before it would be level with the plain. "How much longer do you think?" asked one, staring thoughtfully down at the ditch.

"Not long," replied Yan. "A few days at most, unless it rains. That's what we need now – rain to soften the plain and bog down their carts." The others nodded in agreement. They all looked up to Yan. Apart from throwing a spear or firing an arrow, he was the only one to have been engaged in combat with the enemy. He had slain two Lion-men single-handedly in close combat, had been wounded himself and had escaped and lived to tell the tale. This gave him great esteem in their eyes, and they often asked him about things of which he knew no more or even less than themselves. At first, he was embarrassed by this. After all, everything he had done he had done out of fear. He had slain his enemies in terror to save himself, and somehow, he felt guilty that he had survived and his friend had died. Each time the Lion-men approached the wall, he felt the same terror again, but he controlled himself and did not show his fear to his companions. It was important to him what others thought, and gradually, he found himself trying to live up to their expectations. So now when they asked his opinion, he answered with great confidence although inside he felt hollow and fearful.

"It's strange there's been no action yet," said another of Yan's companions. "They're usually here by now. Do you think they're giving us a day off?" But even as he spoke, they noticed movement within Agon's camp. At first, sections of barricades were drawn aside as usual but then, to their astonishment, the tall, wooden siege towers which they had watched growing higher and higher over the previous weeks, slowly began to move forward across the plain. At the same time, another construction, which had not been visible before, emerged onto the Great Way and slowly trundled towards the main gates. It was a huge battering ram fastened onto a wheeled trellis. Its nose was tapered but blunt and clad in iron. Yan's stomach flipped. His companions, frightened and excited, were already blowing on their horns to sound warning of the attack, and they were joined by a chorus of other horns all around the city.

"Why are they attacking now?" Yan was asked. "The ditch isn't full yet." Yan shrugged – this time he had no answer. As the ram trundled towards the gate, it seemed there could be only one possible outcome – its front wheels would fall into the ditch, burying its nose into the earth. It just did not make sense.

***

Iordic stretched his legs ever so slightly, quietly, then his arms and finally his neck, pushing his head very carefully backwards into the cold, damp ground. This would be his last chance to move his stiff, aching limbs whilst the night still hid him. He knew from the changing of the watch on the walls above him that dawn was near, and then he must be as motionless as the corpses that surrounded him until it was time to act…

He had lain in the ditch all night, feigning death. Somewhere within a few yards of him were others playing the same macabre game, hopefully at least four, but possibly as many as six. During the long night he had heard one of them move, and though the noise was only slight, in the dead of the night it sounded like a drum roll to Iordic. Surely, they could hear it on the walls? But no one came; no one threw down an exploratory spear; and after several nerve-stretching minutes, he relaxed again.

That night seemed interminable, and it gave Iordic plenty of time to think and to reflect on the events that had brought him here, to a cold, damp ditch under the walls of Trion. Already he had broken his promise to his woman back in the valley, not to take undue risks, to be careful, to make sure that he returned to care for his one remaining child. But when Agon had asked for volunteers for a task that could end the siege in hours rather than months, he had stepped forward without thinking – that was his problem, he was too impulsive. It was the idea of ending this thing quickly and getting home that had driven him forward, without waiting to assess the risks. Now, here he was in about the most dangerous place he could be, and for what? When he could have let someone else do this and still got home before winter.

It was not that he felt any great loyalty to Agon; in fact he disliked and feared him. But the last years had been disastrous, a poor crop followed by a harsh winter. His second child had died like many others, weakened by famine, killed by fever. Now another poor crop and another winter to come… he could not bear the thought of losing another child. Agon had promised them everything: "If we bring back the Lion, which was stolen from us, then the valleys will be fertile again; our people will prosper; and bad fortune will never return. We will flourish like the people of Trion!"

Of course, people had heard such talk before from other rash and ambitious leaders. But this Agon was different – he was wily and ruthless and had ways of winning friends and cowering his opponents. With a band of his closest followers, he had ambushed caravans of traders and stolen their food, some of it heading south from Trion. Sometimes he disappeared for weeks without end and then returned with a string of horses laden with food which he would distribute amongst the people, winning their friendship and support. He would even take food to neighbouring tribes and say proudly, "See, whilst your leaders sit timidly at home preaching patience and prudence, I, Agon, bring you food!" Rumours that he butchered all those he stole from even when they did not resist, did not prevent people from taking his food to feed themselves or a malnourished child. To those who opposed him, he taunted them, saying, "And what have you done for your people? Before you speak you should join me on my next trip and see what risks I take to bring these things." Those who did not accept his invitation were branded as cowards, and those who did often did not return – they met with an unfortunate accident or were mysteriously unlucky in combat. Soon Agon was both feared and revered.

Even so, it was not easy to persuade people to attack Trion. Had this not been tried many times before and always ended in disaster? Ah, but this time would be different, claimed Agon, because this time he had a plan – a plan that could not fail. Of course, he could not tell anybody what this plan was because its success depended upon its complete secrecy and 'the enemy has eyes and ears everywhere'. This was an extremely cunning ploy by Agon, for how could anyone criticise a plan they knew nothing of? "But how do we know that it cannot fail?" some asked.

"Have I ever failed you?" he replied. By using such rhetoric, and the skilful deployment of fear and rewards, he won over one tribe then another until none dared to oppose him openly.

Now here he was, Iordic, impulsive fool, a part of Agon's plan, lying in the cold ditch. But was this the plan? The plan that could not fail? If so, Iordic was not impressed; he could think of a dozen ways in which it could fail. Or was this merely a minor stratagem within the plan, something whose success or failure was not crucial? But there was no point in thinking about that now – there was light in the sky and the sight of it made Iordic's palms sweat and his heart race. He held his body rigid, not daring to move a muscle.

An age seemed to pass before he heard the first sounds of the attack – first shouting and horns blowing on the wall above him, then the trundling and creaking of siege machines being pushed across the plain to the solemn, slow beat of a drum keeping Agon's army in time. The drum beat gathered pace; the noise of the approaching army grew to a crescendo; and then at last – the signal! – a shrieking, high-pitched whistle flying across the plain like a stricken, fearsome bird of prey.

Iordic leapt to his feet, surprised, almost, that his stiff, aching limbs still obeyed him. Surprised, too, that his companions rose around him, like dead men out of the earth. Quickly, they did what they had practised so much before: two long shields slotted together, one long spear run through their handles to strengthen them, one half of a primitive bridge thus formed, quickly hoisted across the top of the ditch and completed by another. Two shield planks bridging the ditch, each to take one set of wheels of the huge ram now hurtling towards them. Huddled underneath were the makers of this crude construction, bracing their remaining spears between the earth and the shields, straining every muscle to hold the bridge. It only had to hold for one second – just long enough for the ram to make its first and final journey across the ditch and into the gate.

But a second is a long time when you are a human bridge and when success or failure may bring the same reward: a violent, painful death.

Bang! The front wheels hit the bridge. Miracle! They had managed to line up the wheels with the bridge as planned.

Crack! One of the shields split.

Bang! The rear wheels hit the bridge.

Smash! The shields folded in the middle; the spears splinted; Iordic and his companions fell into the ditch, showered with the remains of their bridge.

Thud! The rear wheels hit the far edge of the ditch, but they did not stop there; the momentum of the ram was enough to carry it forward…

Boom! Crash! The ram smashed through the outer gates of Trion and stopped.

***

Yan stood mesmerised on the wall. He had just seen what appeared to be sheer folly transformed into a brilliant tactical plan in a few seconds. The outer gate of the city had been smashed open and Agon's army were now pouring across the partially filled ditch to seize the ram and with it beat down the inner gate. As for the siege towers, instead of falling into the ditch, they had been cunningly designed to lean forward across the ditch as their front wheels rolled into it, thus forming huge, gently inclined ladders for the Lion-men to scale up to the walls. Agon had thus been able to attack the city before its defenders thought he was ready and so achieve what all military commanders desire above all else: surprise.

"What shall we do?" asked one of his companions, nervously. Yan hesitated – what should they do? Go to the nearest siege tower or go to the gate? He opened his mouth as if to answer but no words came out – his mind had been overwhelmed by fear and confusion. Fortunately, he was rescued; a firm hand gripped his shoulder and a voice issued instructions: "You men, get down to that siege tower and fight, don't gawk! Yan, come with me!"

Yan turned to see Tormon already hurrying on in front of him along the wall towards the gate, issuing orders to soldiers below as he went. "You lot," he yelled, "get up here and go to the nearest siege tower and fight! Han – don't come up here with that leg of yours. Stay at the bottom of the steps and deal with any men that get down there." Han grunted, hauling his double-handed mace – his preferred weapon – over his shoulder.

The walls now seemed alive with soldiers hurrying to contain the Lion-men on the siege towers. Archers gathered in throngs around their leaders. Some hurried to the base of the walls opposite the towers to pick off any Lion-men that broke through; others were already taking up position on the walls to fire flaming arrows into the towers to set them alight.

They were soon above the gate and Tormon opened the door that led into a chamber over the tunnel between the inner and outer gates. The floor was honeycombed with holes, and through them, Yan could clearly see the Lion-men below clearing the debris of the smashed gate away from the ram. He had never been in this chamber before and had often wondered what it was for. In the centre of the chamber was a large metal cauldron with a spout protruding from the lip. It was supported between two stands fastened to the floor and attached to each side of it was a long, lever-like handle.

"Here, put these on," ordered Tormon, handing him a large helmet and a pair of thick, heavy gloves. The helmet completely covered his head, and he could see only dimly through a dark, semi-transparent material which covered his eyes. "Now do as I do," said the now muffled voice of Tormon. "Carefully and slowly, and once the liquid starts to pour, try not to breathe until we leave the chamber."

They each took one of the handles and slowly began to tip the cauldron. As they did so, they heard the first blow of the ram upon the inner gate. It seemed to make little impact, but what would be the result after twenty, or a hundred, or a thousand such blows? Would the inner gates still hold? Would the power of the Lion-Image shatter the ram into a thousand pieces?

As the cauldron tipped, Yan could dimly see beneath it a metal-lined basin-like indentation in the floor, and spreading out from it, in every direction, metal-lined grooves cut deep into the stone, leading to every hole in the floor of the chamber. A thin stream of sparkling silver liquid issued from the spout and fell into the basin. It ran in every direction along the grooves deep in the stone several inches below their feet, forming a huge silver web across the floor.

At first, nothing happened. The ram struck the gate a second time.

Then, slowly, it began: first one scream, then another. Then the screams became more frantic and higher-pitched. Not the screams of the wounded and the dying but screams of absolute terror so strange and piercing that one could not tell if they were of man, woman or beast. Then, rising up through the holes in the chamber, the smell of burning flesh – human flesh – borne in an acrid stinging smoke that pricked Yan's eyes even through his helmet. It was as though this lever, which Yan gripped tightly in his gloved hands, had prised open the gates of hell, and through the helmet and the smoke and the holes in the floor Yan could dimly see below him the tortured forms of demons burning and choking and slashing wildly at each other in their futile efforts to escape.

He remembered Tormon's warning not to breathe until they left the chamber. This, coupled with the fearful scenes and noise from below, filled Yan with panic. His whole body shook and sweated uncontrollably; his lungs screamed for air – clear, pure air. Yet still they poured. Until, at last, he felt Tormon pulling back on the cauldron, and slowly they righted it. Then, not waiting for Tormon's instruction, Yan flung himself through the door, tearing off his helmet and swallowing lungs full of air as he leaned exhausted against the wall.

Down below, around the gates, the Lion-men's moment of triumph as they smashed through the outer gate was quickly turned into terror and confusion. At first, as the deadly liquid rained down upon them, they had tried to protect themselves by raising their shields above their heads. But the liquid burnt straight through their shields as though they were made of straw; burnt straight through their flesh to the very bone; burnt straight through their boots, searing through their feet. Some, naturally, looked up to see what was happening and the liquid, dropping into their eyes, burning through to their skulls, drove them crazy with pain. This was not an enemy they could fight with shields and swords; this was liquid death and agony raining down upon them.

Utter chaos and confusion followed. They turned to flee the tunnel, but those outside were still surging forward trying to get in, preventing their escape. Then a noxious gas arose as the liquid began to vaporise, burning their eyes and choking their lungs. They grew desperate and began to hack and slash at their own kind to get out. Some emerged from the tunnel bearing dreadful gaping wounds, spitting blood and cutting furiously in all directions, killing many of their own men. Soon, panic spread through all of Agon's army around the gate, and the attack turned into a rout as arrows poured down on them from the walls.

The attack on the gate had failed, but the battle was not yet over. At several points around the city, the Lion-men from the siege towers had managed to establish themselves on the walls. These now had to be repulsed and the towers destroyed before the Lion-men could get onto the walls in sufficient numbers to overrun the city. These were desperate hours for Trion, but with the pressure relieved on the gate, Tormon was able to concentrate enough soldiers on each tower to eventually overcome it.

High above the city, from their favoured vantage points, those citizens not involved in the fighting had watched the battle ebb and flow, groaning with fear and despair when things seemed to be going badly, cheering with relief as they went well. But when the battle was over and won, they did not feel the elation that usually comes with victory. Their city bore the scars of battle. The burnt-out shells of siege towers still clung to the walls like giant stick insects struck dead by the unexpected onset of winter. Protruding from the gate they could see the tail end of the once mighty battering ram, lying on its side, its carriage now burnt and broken, a discarded toy, but still a reminder of what could have happened. Worse still, they all knew that many more of their citizens had died that day than in all the previous weeks of the siege added together, and those who had not personally witnessed the death of one they cherished feared the news that may await them when they returned home.

Zeth had watched the battle ebb and flow around the city. He too had felt the fear and relief. For him, it was as though he were watching it for the second time, as though he were seeing what he had once dreamed. For had he not foreseen this already; had he not experienced the bitterness of victory as well as of defeat before a blow had been struck, before Agon's army had even arrived? But he had also seen something new. He had seen the carnage at the gate, and it had horrified and troubled him. For if Fidias were right, and the Lion-men were just like him… to use such a vile, obscene substance… yet was it not necessary, absolutely necessary to save the city? Perhaps it was… yet why was it that the use of such a thing had become the only solution? And where had this substance come from, this rain of terror against which no human being could defend themself? To that there could be only one answer – it had come from the same source that had brought Zeth so many wonderful things: his knowledge of the fixed and wandering stars, his love of the mysteries of numbers, his knowledge of light and earth and air and, above all, the making of images – it had come from the Houses of Learning. This did not seem right, that the Houses of Learning, which could produce so much that was difficult, and ingenious, and wonderful, should also produce this one obscene solution.

Chapter Seven

Taking Stock

Thea looked down the council table. There were two empty chairs, each a reminder of what was happening to her city – one councillor had been slain and another wounded in the first serious battle of the siege. Her hair, which before had been jet black, was already flecked with grey. Her brow, once clear and smooth, was now slightly furrowed. Never had the burden of office been greater. She hoped that this first great battle would be the last and that Agon, his surprise attack having failed, would retreat, leaving her city in peace. For she felt the death of every citizen, the orphaning of every child, to be a silent rebuke to her and her government. Would not a wiser leader have found a way to prevent this madness?

"Councillors," she began, "we have won a great battle – let us hope it is the last. We have, alas, lost many of our brave citizens, but Agon has suffered far greater losses, and his machines, the fruit of much labour, have been destroyed. Winter is almost here and his soldiers, who have suffered much already, must surely grow restless for their homes. Is the war won? What need we do next? I await your counsel."

An elderly councillor rose to reply. He stooped but his voice was strong and brimming with confidence as he spoke:

"Agon has failed. It was clear when they first appeared that he did not have enough men to sustain a prolonged siege, and we wondered at his folly. Now we know that his plan was to take the city quickly with this cunning surprise attack using these artfully contrived machines, and he almost succeeded. But thanks to the quick thinking and action of our Captain of the Guard and the ingenuity of our Houses of Learning, his plan has failed. Now the winter stretches before Agon's wounded army, which must surely soon lose faith in its leader. Let us hasten this process. Let us celebrate our victory with a great festival. Let us light fires and make music in the market square. Let us organise games in celebration. But most of all, let us bring food out of the stores and cook it in the open air and drive Agon's army, shivering and hungry, out on the open plain, mad with envy and despair."

He sat. Some murmured their approval. Then, as silence fell upon the council, Tormon felt the eyes of many councillors upon him, including those of Thea, so that he felt compelled to speak. He sighed deeply, then said:

"I fear that these are not the words you wish to hear, so I hesitate to utter them, but I would be failing in my duty not to counsel caution. Agon's army, though weakened, is still intact. Though it may not be strong enough to take the city, it still outnumbers us, and while it remains at our gates, we must remain within the walls. It would be folly now to consume what is in the stores, what is vital to our survival. We have defeated his first major attack – that is all. It was an attempt to take the city quickly, a brilliant attempt

68

that almost succeeded. This man is clever, too clever to have gambled everything on this first attack which could have failed for many reasons. We have wounded his army, maybe demoralised them; maybe they will lose heart and melt away. But until they do, we must stand firm, do nothing rash, conserve our supplies, be patient."

A third councillor, sitting at the right hand of the first who spoke, now rose:

"We respect the counsel of our noble captain who is a cautious man always alert to every possible danger, and how often has his cautious advice proved right?! But I fear on this occasion that he overestimates our enemy. Tormon flatters Agon if he thinks that he possesses the same cautious foresight and wisdom as himself. We must remember who we are dealing with. These people are savages; they have no foresight, no long-term strategy, a few clever tricks, yes, but that is all. Well, their tricks have failed as we knew they must. Now it is time to sweep them from our gates like autumn leaves. I say we have a great feast to show the Lion-men how little their presence concerns us and then, whilst they are driven mad with hunger and envy, we should launch a surprise attack. The time for cowering behind our walls is over! How many will stand and fight? None, I tell you! They will flee back to their valleys and trouble us no more."

"But this is madness!" blurted out Han, who could contain himself no longer. "Whilst we have the walls between ourselves and Agon's army, they lose two or three men for every one of ours. Yet you call upon us to throw away our chief advantage and fight them in the open where our losses must be much greater. No, if their morale is as low as you say, then the winter will do our work for us with little loss of life, and if it isn't, then to attack is folly."

"And what of the Lion?" asked another councillor. "It will protect us within the walls, but if we go out onto the plain, we leave its protection behind." This last remark produced a strange, uncomfortable silence. Since the siege had begun, little had been said of the Lion-Image and its reputed powers. It had seemed somehow irrelevant to the day-to-day concerns of the besieged citizens, and some had even asked what use the Lion-Image was when it protected the walls of Trion but did not prevent its citizens from being picked off one at a time or from gradually dying through hunger or boredom.

Tormon glanced at the Lion-Image – yes, it was still beautiful, but somehow it no longer seemed so powerful and awesome. Thea now turned to him to speak once more: "Our council seems divided, Tormon, but can you tell us what it is that you fear? Agon cannot possibly take the city with the forces now left at his disposal, and he cannot possibly expect his soldiers to last through the winter on the open plain. What possible strategy can he have?"

Tormon looked troubled. He had been asked the question which he did not want to answer, but after a short silence, he spoke:

"I do not know. I cannot read his mind. But who guessed when the great ram came rolling across the plain that a bridge would rise up out of the earth to carry it crashing into our gates? None. And who can guess, now that his army is too weak to take the city by storm and the winter draws on, what his plans may be? He has had a long time to plan this siege, and I cannot believe that he risked everything on the success of this first ingenious attack. You say that I overestimate him. Maybe so, but at least let us wait a while and observe the mood in his camp, watch to see what his next move will be before we do anything rash."

The debate continued, ebbing and flowing between those who, buoyed up by the failure of Agon's first assault, wanted to take the initiative and hasten the end of the siege, and those, like Tormon, who urged caution, to sit and wait… wait for the winter to gnaw the bones of their enemies and sap their will. And who can say who was right and who was wrong, for in the end all roads may lead to disaster. All that we know is that, finally, a compromise was reached, and it was decided that there should be a celebration of the victory with music and sporting events to raise the morale of the besieged citizens, but there was only to be a small increase in their allotted daily rations and there were to be no daring surprise attacks on Agon's army.

Chapter Eight

Tales by Firelight

The following day, in accordance with decrees issued by the council, a festival was held. In the centre of the market square, several oxen were slain and slowly roasted over great fires fuelled partly by the remains of the siege towers which had been hauled over the walls the night before. Around these fires, a host of sporting events took place: archery and spear-throwing contests, races, wrestling matches and acrobatics, some performed on horseback. The whole festival was accompanied by fanfares and singing so that there could be no doubt in the minds of the Lion-men what was happening inside the city. Tormon had been careful to post a watch around the city walls to guard against a surprise attack, but nothing stirred within Agon's camp.

As daylight began to fail and the sporting events drew to an end, some oxen were carved, and the prime cuts given to soldiers, but all the citizens of Trion tasted meat for the first time in many weeks. Then, smaller fires were lit all around the market square and people huddled round them and roasted chestnuts and listened to the storytellers. And how sweet it was, after so much fear and frugal living, to sit before the fire with one's stomach filled with meat, to dance the hot chestnuts between your hands and to listen to the soft, intoxicating tones of the storyteller!

Zeth sat by one of these fires. He loved to hear the stories as much as anyone in Trion, especially at night-time in front of the fire. This storyteller was a particularly good one. At times he leaned forward, his eyes gleaming with excitement, his face lit up by the firelight. Sometimes his eyes would catch Zeth's, holding them almost in a spell for a few seconds, then they would release him and flit quickly to another listener. Sometimes he simply stared, trance-like, into the fire as though he were hearing the story himself for the first time, as though it were being dictated to him by another voice far away. Then, suddenly, he would sit back, disappearing into shadow, but all the time his voice continued, rising and falling gently, holding them spellbound until he was done.

And what fascinating and comforting stories he told! Stories that they all knew but which they all loved to hear again and again, each time told in a different way, each time with some added detail or nuance that they had not heard before. Stories of the founding of Trion…

"… and Los and his followers came down from the mountains and saw the Plain of Trion stretched before them, and it was empty of all living things and barren. But Los scooped up a handful of earth and let it fall between his fingers and saw that it was good. Then he strode out onto the plain and walked for several days until he and his followers came to its very centre. There they came upon a rock, smooth and hard, and with a fine texture. Los sat himself upon the ground and took from his pocket the instruments of his art, the hammer and the chisel, and fashioned the rock into an image of great power: the Image of the Lion. Then Los took his staff and marked upon the earth a great circle with the Lion-Image as its centre and so circumscribed the limits of the city which was to be called, Trion!"

Here the storyteller rose to his feet as he said, with trembling voice, "Then Los declared that for as long as the Lion-Image lies at the heart of the city, none that enters it can be an enemy!" At this, the listeners leapt to their feet, joining the storyteller and cheering at the sound of such comforting words.

But Zeth did not; he sat rooted to the ground, pondering on what he had heard. For it occurred to Zeth, who had heard these words many times before, that there was more than one way in which they could be interpreted. Before, he had always taken them to mean what everyone else thought them to mean: that the power of the Lion-Image would always keep out their enemies. But what did Los mean by the heart of the city? And did 'none that enter it can be an enemy' mean the same as 'no enemy can enter the city'? And what of the walls? There was no mention of them, only a line drawn in the earth. These questions had never occurred to him before, but now they burned into his mind with such an intense urgency that he blurted out unintentionally: "But what of the walls?"

There was silence as everyone turned to this boy who had so rudely interrupted the storyteller. The storyteller looked at him, surprised, and asked, "What of the walls?"

Zeth felt foolish and embarrassed at his outburst but felt forced to explain: "Well…" he stammered, "there were no walls when Los made the Lion-Image. Was the city protected even before the walls were built? And who built the walls, and when?"

There was a stunned silence. It was as though someone had asked, "What is the Sun's favourite day?" or "What colour is archery?" They were simply questions that did not make sense to ask of the stories. Of course, young children asked foolish questions, but then their parents would simply laugh and invent make-believe answers. But this was different – in a boy of Zeth's age such questions could only indicate madness or stupidity or an attempt to make fun of the storyteller. A murmur of disapproval ran through the crowd. Then one man shouted out, "But of course Los built the walls; that is why he made the line, to show where the walls should be."

"But," objected Zeth, "the stories tell us that after Los made the Lion-Image and drew the line in the earth, he and his followers built the Houses of Learning in which to practise the arts and sciences they brought with them from over the mountains and which were to make Trion great. If Los built the walls, surely, he would have built them after he had drawn the line and before they built the Houses of Learning, but the stories do not say that; the stories say—"

"Peace!" interrupted the storyteller, holding up his hand in protest. "Peace! We are here to tell the stories, not to discuss them. The stories are not witnesses at a tryal to be cross-examined. They are our comforters in hard times; our light during the long, dark nights. Listen and be comforted! Listen, then sleep." And as if to underline his words, the fire suddenly crackled and snapped.

The crowd now silenced, the storyteller continued, "And the first house to be built was the House of Images…"

Zeth wandered away towards home, deeply troubled and cursing silently his ever-troubled mind which was always thinking, never able to lose itself as others did in the comfort of stories and firelight.

Chapter Nine

Agon's Plan Revealed

After the festival, a strange mood fell over the city. The festival had felt like the end of something or the beginning of something. In fact, it was neither the end nor the beginning of anything. Events continued exactly as they had before the battle: small groups of Lion-men would periodically emerge from Agon's camp, loose a few arrows over the wall, then ride away again. The besieging army showed no signs of moving or changing its tactics but continued as before, week after week, after week.

The mood in the city turned from jubilation to quiet despair. Soon the heroic victory seemed nothing more than a bright spark in a sea of interminable gloom.

Meanwhile, the winter closed in; a cold wind blew from the east and the days began to grow shorter. Cold rain fell on the field of Trion, drenching the mournful wrecks of siege engines left abandoned around the walls and making the passage of others across the ground between the walls and Agon's camp impossible.

In theory, this should have favoured the citizens of Trion, sheltered within their city and with sufficient food and fuel to see them through the winter. Agon's army, meanwhile, shivered in makeshift shelters out on the plain. But to the besieged citizens of Trion, bored and uncertain within their walls, observing Agon's apparently immovable army, it did not seem so.

Within Agon's camp, matters were much worse. The Lion-men froze and shivered in the cold, wet wind. Food rations were barely sufficient, and sickness began to spread slowly throughout the army. But worst of all was the sense of futility that hung over them since the assault on the city had failed. Was that the great plan? Had it failed? Nobody seemed to know except Agon, who was telling them nothing. How could they survive through the winter out on the plain and hope to take a city whose walls seemed so high and strong and well defended? Would they ever see their homes again or die of cold and sickness out here on the sodden plain?

Still, they were not left idle. Trees had to be felled to construct more siege engines and scaling ladders, endless ladders – it seemed that almost every man would have his own ladder. As the nearest trees had already been felled, the journeys to and fro became longer. With the cold and hunger and labour, the men became weaker and more demoralised – what could Agon be thinking of? This army would be too weak even to march home long before the siege would force the city of Trion to surrender. As for another full-scale assault upon the city, it seemed hopeless.

Even so, there were enough fit Lion-men to continue harassing the city, and the besieged citizens could only guess at the conditions in Agon's camp. Agon was careful to keep his best troops well fed and rested – those who had served him since the beginning – and it was these that he used to keep up the pressure on Trion so that the soldiers on the walls had no inkling of the state of health of the bulk of Agon's army.

Iordic had survived the battle at the gates. Fortunately for him, being in the bottom of the ditch, he had no chance of being amongst the first to enter the shattered gates. But he had witnessed the carnage at close quarters and still woke at night sweating with the terror of it. However, because he had volunteered for the hazardous task of being part of the human bridge, he had been rewarded by being promoted into Agon's elite, and as such received better rations and lighter duties. He would soon discover that this was a very mixed blessing. For the time being, however, he considered himself fortunate and, being good at heart, felt obliged to share some of his good fortune with his comrades.

The winter solstice came and went, and as the days began to lengthen, the weather became even more brutal; temperatures fell below freezing at night and the ground became rock hard. The rain ceased, but occasionally there were flurries of snow and hail. There was discontent amongst the Lion-men.

Iordic noticed strange things happening in the camp. As the carts that brought their rations from the river valleys returned, they were no longer sent back empty: more and more sick and wounded men were put in them and returned to their homes. At first, there was nothing odd in this – the wounded had always been sent back; they were no longer of any use to Agon and were a burden on the fit and well. It became apparent, however, that even the slightly wounded or enfeebled were being sent back, and soon the number of men left in the camp began to fall alarmingly. Iordic saw many of his friends depart, some of whom were merely tired and drained by the conditions. He envied them and rued his luck – because of his favoured position, he remained fit and well and so remained.

These events gave rise to much speculation amongst the Lion-men. The most persistent rumour being that Agon was planning to abandon the siege. But why do it by stealth? Why not simply strike camp and leave the Plain of Trion en masse? And why did the construction of ladders and siege engines continue unabated?

The citizens of Trion were completely ignorant of what was happening in Agon's camp. They could not see beyond the ramshackle makeshift defences that the Lion-men had built to impede any attempt at a surprise attack from the city. They could see siege engines growing out of the ground within the camp and of course they suffered the continuous harrying by riders on horseback. Until one day, just before dawn, Agon ordered all his remaining men to leave the camp and to retreat beyond the skyline, beyond the perplexed eyes of the soldiers on the walls of Trion, leaving the camp deserted except for the looming structures of abandoned siege engines standing like eerie sentinels, waiting silently, but for what?

***

"It's a trick – it must be!" urged the councillor next to Han. "Why would they build all those siege engines and then desert them?"

"Why indeed?" asked another. "And what is the trick? There are no Lion-men within sight. What is to stop us from destroying the siege engines and razing the remains of Agon's camp to the ground?"

"As soon as we open the gates, they will appear," replied the first. "Just as they rose out of the ditch to make a bridge for the ram."

"That was a handful of men," replied the second. "How could they hide an entire army?"

The council was in confusion. Even Tormon was perplexed. There were many possible explanations for why Agon had deserted his camp. But there was no clear evidence to indicate which was the correct one. Had his men simply had enough and deserted? Or was it part of another cunning deception? Caution was needed. What mattered was not that the camp had been abandoned but what to do now that it had been.

"We must wait a day," said Tormon. "We must wait a day and a night and then, and only then, send a small party out to investigate. And if there is no immediate danger, that small party should set fire to the siege engines and raze them to the ground."

"Tormon seems most definite in his council," said Thea. "Please," she continued, "explain your reasoning – why tomorrow? Why not today, or in a week, or a month?"

"No one would take an entire army – an army that has been exhausted by cold and battle and labour through half a winter – away from its only shelter overnight, even for one night. Even Agon is not fool enough to do that – it would debilitate his troops even further. No, they are gone for good, or they will be back very soon. They are trying to tempt us out now or not at all. They have either gone or it is another devilish trap that must be sprung immediately or never. Or it is something else, something I cannot fathom. But if they do not return tomorrow, it would be foolish to leave the means of our destruction lying on our doorstep for another army to use."

Tormon did not realise how near he was to the truth and yet how far he was from understanding Agon's tactics. Yet once again, his practical logic seemed unassailable. So, after further brief discussion, it was decided to follow Tormon's council and wait to see what the next twenty-four hours would bring. Just one day. But in less than a day, a grave blow was dealt to the defenders of Trion – a blow that was struck without a single arrow being fired, without a single sword being lifted, or a single spear being thrown.

***

Iordic was a foot soldier, so he marched briskly behind the mounted troops away from Trion. But where were they going? He knew in his heart that they were not going home; Agon would not give up Trion so easily and he seemed to be in a good, almost exultant, mood – he certainly did not have the demeanour of a defeated man. They marched for several hours, until the city of Trion disappeared over the horizon. But he had noticed that Agon had left behind a few men with fast horses hidden in a small copse still just within sight of the city.

The army was halted and ordered to rest. It was less than half of its original size and many of those who remained looked less than fit for war. As they rested, the least fit were weeded out, given a few carts full of provisions and told to continue home. The army was now about a third of its original size. All that remained were Agon's elite forces and those few whose constitutions had been strong enough to see them through the worst of the winter fully fit and well.

Iordic settled down to eat a meal of salted beef and raw carrot, watching those fortunate enough to be unfit wend their way down the long, sloping escarpment away from Trion towards the hills and the river valleys that were their home. He had just finished when he noticed some movement right on the horizon beyond the bedraggled runt of Agon's army. Gradually, the movement grew more pronounced and larger, signifying that whatever it was, it was coming towards him. Soon it was clear that it was a large body of men and horses moving briskly and directly in their direction. Iordic was alarmed – could this be a trap? An army from Trion sent out to encircle them? But no – he could see Agon and his generals watching too, and they seemed unperturbed, not even surprised. Now every soldier was on his feet, watching anxiously as it became clear that a large army was closing on them, an army almost as large as Agon's original army had been.

As they drew near, it was obvious who they were: Lion-men from those tribes who had not sworn their allegiance to Agon, or so it had seemed. Now Agon rode forward to meet their leaders. They embraced, and a few words were exchanged. Iordic looked in awe – here was a new army, fresh and well supplied. All the difficult work of the siege had been done for them – the ditch had been filled, the outer gates breached, the ladders and siege engines built and the back of winter broken. Now with a new army fresh to the field, surely Agon could not but succeed. So, this was the great plan: to weaken Trion with half his force whilst keeping the other half fresh in reserve, safe from the ravages of winter – simple but effective.

***

In Trion, the sight of the plain devoid of Lion-men was too much for the citizens. At first, all thought it was a trick, but as the hours rolled by and still there was not the slightest sign of movement around Agon's camp, people gave way to what they most wanted to believe: that the spirit of Agon's army had been broken and that the siege was over. Spontaneous celebrations broke out all over the city; there was laughter and dancing in the streets and, more alarmingly, some people began to eat up their rations and to fail to turn up for guard duty on the walls. Within a few hours, all the coiled-up tension within the city had been unwound, and with it the discipline which the siege had imposed was undermined.

Tormon grew increasingly concerned and ordered the reading of edicts in every quarter, urging people to attend to their duties and to stick to their rations until it was certain that the siege was over, but amidst the revelry and excitement, it was difficult to get people's attention and even harder to be taken seriously. As a last desperate measure, he asked the council to order the blowing of the horn – something only done to signify great and imminent danger. "Our guard is down," he argued. "Agon may not be far away – if this is a trick, we have already fallen for it." The council reluctantly agreed.

As the horn was lifted once again shoulder-high and bellowed its mournful notes across the city in the fading grey light of another winter's day, the citizens of Trion stopped whatever they were doing and stood frozen in their tracks, brought to their senses at last. As chance would have it, no reason was needed to be given for its sounding, for as they looked up in fear towards the watchtower, the soldiers there were already pointing across the plain, their trembling fingers indicating Agon's return. Soon, it was clear that Agon had returned with reinforcements and that his army was larger than before. The effect of such a turnaround on the morale of the citizens was devastating – from the heights of exultation they were plunged into the depths of despair. Many simply sank down to their knees and wept; others wandered aimlessly in shock, unable to believe what had happened.

Agon did not miss his opportunity – he knew that this was the right time to strike, and he immediately launched a ferocious attack on the city. His new army was fresh and strong, and it was facing a disorganised and unprepared foe. The siege engines were pushed to within yards of the wall before a single arrow had been fired in their defence. It was only Tormon's rage that shook the gawking citizens out of their stupor. He raced around the city berating every commander he could find for allowing their charges to have lost their discipline and driving them to gather their troops and get them to the walls.

The first siege tower reached the wall, having met little resistance and disgorged its load of Lion-men who quickly overcame the few defenders on the wall. They swept down the steps and headed for the gates. Tormon had anticipated this and dispatched his own cohort of highly disciplined spearmen to drive them back. Other commanders now led their troops up onto the wall to meet the siege towers. A desperate struggle now took place. The defenders still had the advantage, but only if they could marshal their forces quickly enough before the Lion-men could achieve a breakthrough and open the gates from the inside. No attempt was made to assault the gates from the outside – Agon dared not risk a second horror there.

As the light began to fade, the battle began to swing Trion's way, but their lack of preparation had cost them dear – far more citizens of Trion died in this attack than in the first major assault upon the city, and the shattering of their hopes of an end to the siege was a severe blow to their morale. Although Agon's forces had been driven back a second time, they had won a crucial psychological victory.

Chapter Ten

Sogon the Great Warrior

As the siege entered its second phase, at first nothing much seemed to have changed – the daily probing of the city's defences continued; bands of Lion-men would ride within shooting distance of the walls, discharge their arrows, then swerve quickly out of range of the defenders' missiles. Gradually, the intensity of the attacks increased – Agon would attack several parts of the wall at once, then edge his siege engines a little closer as though about to launch a major assault, only to withdraw them again. He was playing a game of cat and mouse, gradually sapping the strength and resolve of the city's defenders.

Then, when he felt the time was right, he played his trump card: Sogon the Great Warrior.

Sogon was a colossus, standing head and shoulders above his tallest rivals and broad as a barn door. His strength was legendary. It was said he could hold a bullock in its tracks. Agon had made for him a special suit of armour, thicker and heavier than any normal man could wear and fight with, but

Sogon wore it lightly and moved with the ease and heft of a war horse. One kick from Sogon would send a man flying, one thrust of his shield would send him flat on his back, and when he brought down his huge blade, no armour could turn it.

Agon had first met him when visiting one of the smaller tribes two years before his assault on Trion. He was standing beside the tribe's chief, arms folded, huge and terrifying. Immediately, Agon saw his potential. What a man to have by your side – who would dare defy you?

Agon was up to his usual tricks, bringing gifts to the tribe – fleeces, mutton, baskets of grain and fruit – laying them at the chief's feet and declaring, "See what Agon brings you! And look at these pitiful few men I have to do it with!" waving to the half dozen men he had brought with him. "How much more could I bring you with a little help?"

Then began the usual, subtle negotiations: "Give me a handful of men and I will bring you more, and more often." Seldom successful at first but difficult to resist after three, four, five visits, each one bringing free gifts, each one making him more popular with the tribe and a hero to some of the younger men who wanted to follow him. The pressure on the chief became irresistible. This time, Agon wanted only one man: Sogon. He walked around him admiringly, flattering him. "What a man! Such a man as this should be clad in fine armour! He should feast on mutton every day! With a man like this, I could bring you great riches."

At first, Sogon and the chief resisted these overtures, but Agon was relentless. His visits became more frequent and the gifts more extravagant. "Let me have him for just a few days – you can have him back if you are not happy. He can return any time he wants." Eventually, Agon, as usual, got his way, and Sogon became part of his marauding army.

He trained him into a fighting machine but used him sparingly; he did not want to lose this prize asset. He had held him back during the first part of the siege of Trion, his human battering ram to be used only when Trion's defences were already weakened. He had made for him specially thickened cuirass, helmet, shoulder plates and greaves, turning him into an almost impenetrable monster. And just to make sure that he did not lose him too soon to a lucky spear or arrow, he assigned two of his elite guards to always fight with him, to guard his flanks and rear.

***

Yan was marching briskly to the east wall with his comrades for another day's duty when he heard the commotion ahead of him. The fighting had already begun, and it was not quite daybreak. Their march turned into a jog, but it was brought to a full stop as they rounded a building and came in sight of the steps up to the walls. On top of the wall, a fierce fight was taking place – a siege engine had made it to the walls and Lion-men had breached the initial defences and were fighting their way to the steps. But what had brought Yan and his comrades to an abrupt halt was the sight of the huge figure in the centre of the melee, the biggest man he had ever seen, blazing in armour and knocking the soldiers of Trion off the wall as though they were children. Despite a wall of shields in front of him, he was pushing forward relentlessly, flanked by his comrades, now only a few yards from the steps.

They watched in horror as Sogon brought down his huge sword on the soldier in front of him, slicing through his shield as though it were straw and almost cutting the hapless soldier in half. He tumbled like a rag doll from the wall. His comrades immediately closed the gap with their shields but retreated now almost to the top of the steps. Sogon moved forward.

There was nothing for it – Yan and his comrades ran up the steps to bolster the defence, but Yan noticed that he was trembling with fear. He was sure he was running to certain death. As they approached, Sogon launched himself at the soldiers in front of him, slaying them mercilessly so that by the time Yan reached the top of the steps, there was no one between him and Sogon. Sogon raised his sword; as he brought it down, Yan stepped aside and used his shield to deflect the blow rather than take its full force. It worked, but before Yan could strike back, Sogon had kicked him full in the chest and sent him tumbling back down the steps. Lying flat on his back, he looked up to see a Lion-man about to launch a spear at him. He rolled under the shelter and shadow of the steps, leaving his shield behind but holding onto his sword. The spear plunged into the ground where he had been, quickly followed by the lifeless bodies of his comrades. He could hear Sogon and his comrades descending the steps and moved further into the shadows, pressing himself against the wall.

Sogon now stood in front of him, flanked by two other Lion-men but looking away from him into the city. Sogon half turned, looking towards the gates. He pointed, indicating where they should go: to the gates. Could nothing stop him now? Was this the end?

As if to answer his unspoken question, Yan heard running feet instantly transformed into a score of archers who appeared from the same direction Yan himself had come from only a minute earlier. Their commander stood to one side of the archers who had stopped abruptly as they found themselves facing Sogon and his guards. Yan recognised her instantly – it was Lelka, the wife of Tormon, Captain of the Guard. She looked stunned for an instant but then recovered herself and shouted, "Arrows!"

The command was followed instantly by the click of wooden shafts against bows. The archers, well drilled, had already formed themselves into two lines, one behind the other.

"Draw," she shouted. The arrows were drawn back along the bows in complete unison.

"Loose!" she yelled. A flight of arrows flew into the Lion-men, who only just had time to raise their shields. None drew blood. Sogon roared and took a step towards the archers, accompanied by the Lion-men flanking him, and raised his sword. Before they could take a second step, Lelka had yelled again: "Arrows! Draw! Loose," and the second line of archers had let loose another salvo.

"Arrows! Draw! Loose!" she yelled yet again.

The Lion-men were now rattled by the incessant rain of arrows, and Sogon's companions were urging him to retreat, but he stood his ground and roared in defiance.

"Arrows!" yelled Lelka. "Draw! Loose!" This time, she drew her own bow and kneeled low, looking for a shot below the shields. She spotted a glimmer of flesh just below Sogon's knee, at the edge of his greave. She drew a deep breath, steadied herself, focused for all her life, for her child's life, and loosed the arrow. It struck home, a glancing strike but enough to bring Sogon down on one knee with the shock and pain. He soon recovered and roared back to his feet, raising his sword and stepping forward. One of his flanking guards had also been hit – a nick in the neck – and both guards now closed their shields in front of Sogon and urged retreat. Behind them, reinforcements were already coming

from the north wall to cut off their retreat to the siege tower
– soon they could be surrounded. The opportunity had
gone.

"Arrows!" shouted Lelka. "Draw! Loose!"

Sogon, now persuaded, retreated up the steps with his
guards, bombarded all the way with flight after flight of
arrows. The crisis was over for now.

Yan watched in awe. He realised that though he could
see Lelka and her archers very clearly, they could not see
him in the deep shadow of the steps. He watched her now
and could see the sweat on her brow, glistening in the rising
sun. She wiped her hand on her tunic and breathed heavily.
Yan marvelled at her courage and composure. Without her
commands, her decisiveness, the archers would probably
have fled faced by Sogon, but she had not given them time
to think, and they had obeyed instinctively, as they had been
drilled.

And he? He had considered attacking Sogon from
behind – he had his sword and the opportunity, but he
lacked the courage. He had stayed, hidden in the shadows,
knowing that if he attacked and failed with his first blow,
then he was a dead man.

When Lelka and her archers moved on, he emerged
from the shadows and joined his comrades on the wall.
Already, he could smell the siege tower burning.

Chapter Eleven

Fidias's Image

Tormon had seen it all from his command post at the top of the watchtower in the centre of the city. It was from here that he directed the defence of Trion. With the aid of his near-glass, he could see every inch of the walls from this one position. At the foot of the tower, he held his reserve: bands of soldiers and archers that he could deploy to any section of the walls that needed reinforcement. So, although Agon's army outnumbered the defenders of Trion, Tormon could outnumber them at any point along the wall by concentrating his forces.

This had always been the secret of Trion's success: knowledge and organisation. The near-glass was a key advantage – a simple tube with shaped glass at either end that enabled Tormon to see clearly what was happening too far away to be seen with the naked eye. It was another wonderful invention made by the Houses of Learning – a closely guarded device whose workings were kept secret from all but a few in Trion. With it, Tormon saw Sogon breach the defences on the wall and immediately dispatched a band of archers to repel him. Only afterwards did he realise that the leader of the band was his own wife, Lelka, and he watched anxiously, realising the great danger he had exposed her to.

At the end of the day, he made a note of the losses on both sides and calculated that more than two Lion-men for every soldier of Trion died that day. It was always so; the defenders held the advantage – the protection of the walls – until the attackers could get close enough. But was the advantage enough? Could he keep defending the walls with the numbers he had before the advantage turned the other way? Numbers and calculations were perhaps more important in war than individual courage or skill. And now there was another number to worry about: the number of sick.

It had started two weeks ago – just a couple of people at first but now increasing every day. A fever that laid people low and unable to fight – not fatal in itself, but fatal if it left the citizens of Trion unable to defend themselves. At the last count, Tormon calculated he had more than a hundred soldiers laid low, unable to fight. He made frequent visits to the House of Healing to ask the healers there to calculate how quickly the fever was spreading, how soon people would recover, how many would be laid low when the numbers peaked. The answer to these questions was more important to his defence of Trion than anything either he or Agon could do.

Tormon was worried. Very, very worried. He paced the floor at home while Lelka sat listening as he went through the numbers with her. There was to be a council meeting the next day and he was rehearsing what he would have to say. Lelka nodded anxiously. Neither was aware that Zeth was listening just outside the door, his ear pressed against the wood. He had long worked out that if he wanted to know what was really going on, he needed to eavesdrop. He listened and understood, and then he did his own calculation – his time in the House of Numbers had not been wasted. Three weeks, he calculated, at the current rate of spread of the fever – after three weeks it would be impossible to defend the city unless those who caught the disease recovered very quickly. Three weeks! Zeth found himself running, running as fast as he could to Fidias.

***

He burst through the door into Fidias's workshop. "Three weeks!" he shouted. "Three weeks – that's all we have left! Three weeks if we're lucky!"

Fidias was busy at work as always but now somewhat hampered by the dressing bound to his right arm, concealing the wound he had suffered on the walls. No one was excused military service, especially now, and it was reluctantly observed that Fidias was a skilled swordsman even though it was also observed that he took no pleasure in killing and could be heard to mutter 'Forgive me' under his breath when dealing a fatal blow.

"Three weeks," said Fidias. "I had better hurry then, if I am to finish this in three weeks."

"But what does it matter if we are all dead in three weeks?" said Zeth.

"If I am to die in three weeks, I can't think of a better way of spending them," replied Fidias. "But why three exactly?"

"Because of the numbers – the numbers that tell us that in three weeks the fever will have made so many of our soldiers ill that we will be overrun."

"Numbers, numbers, yes," said Fidias. "They are like tyrants; you can't argue with them – even when they are wrong."

"But what are we to do?" yelled Zeth. "We can't just let it happen!"

Fidias continued working and said nothing for a while, then: "So, what can we do? Tell me."

"We can take the Lion-Image from the Council Chamber and give it to them – no image is worth another single life!"

"I agree – if you think that giving them the Image would stop the siege, maybe you should try to give it to them – seize it and throw it over the walls."

"But that's impossible – I would never get past the guards at the door."

"You wouldn't have to," said Fidias. "Take one of these instead," and with that he stepped away from his work and drew back a curtain in front of a small alcove in the corner of the room.

It suddenly occurred to Zeth that he had never seen behind the curtain before; he had paid no attention to it, thinking it was just a place where Fidias kept some tools or materials. What he saw now took his breath away. There, arranged on two small shelves, staring at him almost accusingly, were five Lion-Images.

Zeth gasped, speechless, then stepped forward to look closely at them. "It's amazing," he said. "They are identical to the real Lion-Image!"

Fidias laughed, then said, "Then why are they any less real? But you are wrong. Here, look at them – closely, very closely – are they the same?"

Zeth looked closely, moving his eyes from one to another. Yes – they were different. They looked different ever so slightly but he could not see what made them different. Each slightly different in expression, evoking a different nuance of feeling.

"Yes… they are all different… and yet they are all the same…" He looked enquiringly at Fidias.

"Yes," said Fidias, as if to answer Zeth's unspoken question. "I made them all – it's how I learnt when I was young, by copying the great image-makers, and none was greater than Los. But I soon learnt that no two images are ever the same. And yet, if you take one of these and place it on its own," he said, picking one up and placing it on a table, "you would swear it was the Lion-Image of Los."

"Yes, you would…" said Zeth.

Fidias picked up the image and placed it back with the others and closed the curtain. He turned to speak to Zeth, but he was gone.

***

Zeth's mind was racing – his feet were too. He was no longer prepared to stand aside and wait upon events, to see everything and everyone he loved destroyed. He had to do something even if the chances of success were small – a small chance, he reasoned, was better than no chance at all. So, he raced home, slipped quietly into the courtyard and picked Albo's rabbit out of his hutch. He went into the courtyard and pulled one of his mother's arrows from the target.

When he reached the House of Healing it was dusk and already the healers were lighting lanterns. He quickly found his way to Zia's room. She was sitting, half asleep, her head resting against the wall. As Zeth entered, she opened a disinterested eye, then closed it again. But something she had seen must have registered somewhere, because she stirred and opened both her eyes. What she saw was Zeth standing in front of her – in one hand he held Albo's rabbit by its ears, in the other an arrow. She recoiled and pressed herself against the wall. *At last*, thought Zeth, *a reaction.*

"You have to help me, Zia," he yelled. "Albo died because of this stupid rabbit, but unless you help me, a hundred Albos might die. I can't let that happen. You either speak or I will do the only thing I can think of that might make you speak. I will kill this rabbit with this arrow, and I will do it now!"

He didn't wait for a response – he knew that words were useless, but he had an idea that if he made her believe through action… he turned away from her, held the rabbit down upon the table and raised the arrow, holding it like a dagger. As he made to bring it down, Zia's hand reached out and restrained him. He turned to face her and saw that her face was streaming with tears, and from her mouth came a low, agonising moan – the first sound she had made since Albo's death. She slumped back upon the chair and wept and, after a few moments, spoke:

"What do you want?"

"First, I want you to get better," said Zeth. Then he called out, "Healer! Please come."

A confused healer hurried into the room – he was surprised to see Zeth but astonished to see Zia clearly crying.

"She is back with us," said Zeth. "Please feed her and make her strong. I will see you tomorrow, Zia," he said. "Sleep well and get strong. Tomorrow we will talk, and together we will save Trion."

And with that, he scooped the rabbit under his arm and left.

Chapter Twelve

Into the Lion's Den

A flower that is nearly dead, weeks without rain, its leaves drooping and brown at the edges, looks irrecoverable, gone. But add a little water and how quickly it revives – the leaves lift themselves up to receive the light, and within days, the brown has gone, and it is lush and green. So it was with Zia – her tears revived her soul and her body followed. Within a few days, she was almost back to her old self – quick-witted, sharp-tongued. No meadow flower but a cactus.

Zeth visited her every day and told her everything that had happened since that first day of the siege. She asked if she could have Albo's rabbit and Zeth agreed and installed it in her room in its hutch. Whenever he visited, she was sitting stroking the rabbit's ears and staring sadly. But as soon as she saw Zeth, she leapt to life, discarded the rabbit and interrogated him – she wanted to know everything.

A week passed and she asked him: "So, come on, dreamer – what's on your mind? What can I do? You said we would save Trion – how?"

Zeth had not troubled her with what he wanted – he had been waiting until she was stronger, but now he felt the time was right, and even if it wasn't, he felt he could not wait much longer. Every day Agon's attacks grew stronger and more successful – more Lion-men were getting over the walls into the city and creating panic until they were hunted down. Some managed to hide in sheds or deserted houses whose occupants had been slain or were in the House of Healing. They sometimes emerged at night and probed the defences around the main gate, hoping to find a way to open it and let their comrades in.

There was no respite now – night and day there was always risk of attack. Sogon continued his deadly work, used sparingly but creating terror whenever he appeared. As more and more of Trion's soldiers became ill, it was only a matter of time before the city fell.

"I need you to tell me how you got out of the city with Albo," replied Zeth.

"And how is that going to save the city?" asked Zia.

"I have a plan," said Zeth. "Will you promise not to tell anyone if I explain it to you?"

She looked at him. This was not the same dreamer she had known before. He was still a dreamer, an image-maker, but she saw a new steeliness about him, a steeliness that turned dreams into action.

"I will tell you if you let me in on it," she said. "Whatever this plan is, I want to be part of it, to do it with you."

"No," said Zeth. "There is no need. I can do this alone, and it doesn't make sense for two of us to… it would be stupid."

"To what?" demanded Zia. "To do something dangerous? It must be – I love danger; whatever it is, I am doing it with you."

"No, Zia, you can help me by just telling me how to get out of the city, but you can't come with me."

"Then," said Zia, "you will never know how to get out. If you want to get out, for whatever mad, dreamed-up reason, I come with you. That's the deal – take it or leave it. I've lost Albo but now I've got you and you're stuck with me, dreamer!"

***

They met at dusk, by the steps leading down to the river that flowed under Trion. It was, aside perhaps from the walls, Trion's greatest strength. The underground river provided Trion with an endless supply of clean water. Numerous wells throughout the city dipped down into it to access water for the citizens, all placed upstream. Downstream, all the detritus of the city – all the human waste that every city creates – was emptied into the river and carried away under the Plain of Trion. It was perfect, providing both an endless supply of water and a means of carrying away all the city's waste. No one in Trion knew where this blessing started or where it went – nor did they care. It was, indeed, a blessing and doubtless one of the reasons why Los had chosen this spot to build the city.

But the river needed to be kept clear and free – the riverbed needed regular clearing to maintain the flow. Hence the steps leading down to it and the stone walkways that had been constructed along its banks deep underground to enable the river cleaners to do their work. Nobody went down there except them, especially as the foul smell from downstream sometimes made its way to the surface and to the steps where Zeth and Zia now stood.

"Let me see it," said Zia.

Zeth opened the bag slung over his shoulder and took out the Lion-Image he had taken from Fidias's studio. Zia examined it and said, "Yes – it looks just like the real thing. But why should Agon believe it is? Why should he believe that you have managed to get it out of the city to give it to him? Surely, he will think it's just a trick."

"But look at it," said Zeth. "Doesn't it make you feel something, just like the real image? Doesn't it make you feel that it has power?"

"Well," said Zia, "yes, it certainly makes me feel something, but will it fool Agon? And is this really what he wants?"

"It's what he has told his followers that he wants. It's what he has promised them. And if some of them think it is real, that may be enough, enough to create a chance that could lead to a truce, or something. It's a chance; it's better than nothing. But you don't need to come – just show me the way."

"You're mad," said Zia. "But I'm coming. It might get us near enough for me to spit in his eye. Let's go," she said and started down the steps.

When they reached the bottom, Zia took the torch she was carrying and lit it with a fire stick. They turned into the dark tunnel and began walking. The torchlight flickered on the stone walls and arched roof, dripping with moisture from the river that flowed slowly below them. Along the walls, set into shallow alcoves at regular intervals were wrought-iron torch holders used by the river cleaners to light their way. Some still had old, half burnt-out torches left in them. Zia took one out, lit it with her torch and gave it to Zeth, saying, "Here, we can see better with two torches."

Soon, they reached a bend in the river. Just before it, Zia stopped and smiled wickedly at Zeth. She leant back against the wall and reached up to a torch holder above her head. Zeth looked at her, puzzled. "Why have we stopped here?" he asked. She smiled again and pulled down on the torch holder. It moved. She pulled harder and it levered down towards her. At the same time, she pushed her back into the wall and the wall moved too. She pushed harder, using her legs to push it inwards until it was no longer part of the wall but a door, a door opening to a passage.

"But how did you find this?" gasped Zeth. "How could you know that there was a door here and that this torch holder, out of the hundreds down here, would open it?"

"Just luck," said Zia. "I was down here one time following the river cleaners from a safe distance so they wouldn't see me. Then one of them doubled back for some reason – he came round the bend there and I grabbed hold of the torch holder and pushed myself flat to the wall, hoping he wouldn't see me behind the glare of the light, and I felt the wall move behind me. I got out of here as soon as I could, but I could not sleep that night – I had to get back to see what was behind the wall. I was back the next day."

"And you found this passage," said Zeth. "A passage that leads under the city and out beyond the walls?"

"More than that," replied Zia. "Come on – I'll show you." She led on down the narrow passage, brightly lit by the two torches.

They had not gone far when the passage opened up into a large chamber. The two torches now suddenly seemed small and feeble, the brightness of the passage now replaced by the darkness of the chamber. It took a while for Zeth's eyes to adjust, but when they did, he was astonished at what he saw. Wherever the flickering light from the torch illuminated any surface – be it wall or ceiling, or even floor – it revealed images of brilliant, vivid colours.

Zia walked slowly round the circular chamber holding her torch in front or her, illuminating each part of the wall for Zeth to see and smiling at him with such a gleam of pride in her eyes, you would have thought that she had made the images herself. This was her secret, something that only she knew existed, and which she was revealing for the first time to another human being.

The images divided the room into night and day. At first, Zia's torch revealed Trion at night. The Council Chamber could be seen clearly and some of the Houses of Learning, chief amongst them the House of Images, dark but with a bright spot of yellow showing the light burning within. Zeth almost thought he could see Fidias, working away with his chisel. Above the buildings shone the constellations of stars – hundreds of tiny glittering points of light – but all outshone by a brilliant crescent moon.

As the torch passed around the room, night turned to day; the sky became a luminous, clear blue with wispy white scudding clouds and a flock of birds soaring upwards. Below, the Plain of Trion rolled down to the river where a man in a boat was aiming a slingshot at the birds. In another boat, a fisherman was casting his nets. On the plain itself a family lay picnicking and a small boy ran, chasing a dog. Couples walked arm in arm, and down the Great Way a cart trundled along, laden with goods, whilst its driver turned towards the viewer to look at something on the plain behind him.

It was unmistakeable – the man on the cart was a Lion-man, not driving his cart to attack Trion but casually driving down the Great Way as though he belonged there. Then Zeth noticed that some of the figures strolling on the plain were also Lion-men, one with his arm around a woman who was clearly from Trion. Zia's face lit up with delight as she saw the astonishment on Zeth's face.

Each sweep of the torch brought more surprises. On the floor a great circle was drawn, and inside it, two lions faced each other, their backs and tails following the line of the circle, their golden manes filling the room with a warm glow as the torchlight revealed them. Around the outer edge of the circle was a broad band filled with beautiful horses of different coats straddled by bareback riders, laughing as they rode. As Zeth's eyes followed the riders around the room, he saw that they alternated – Lion-man, Trion man, Lion-man, Trion man, not attacking each other but enjoying a friendly sporting contest, racing their horses around a course.

Zeth felt dizzy, intoxicated by the strong bright colours that filled every inch of the room. Then he noticed the most surprising thing of all – there was no gate at the end of the Great Way and no walls to support it – the Lion-man was driving his cart straight into Trion with nothing to bar his way. This was a city without walls, completely at peace with its neighbours.

"This is amazing," Zeth said. "It's as though this was painted yesterday – the colours have not faded at all; everything is perfect!"

"There's no light down here to fade them," said Zia. "And no crowds of people to damage them or pollute them with their breath and heat."

"But how could you know about this and tell no one?" said Zeth. "How could you keep this to yourself?"

"Easy," replied Zia. "Why would I tell anyone? Firstly, I would be in real trouble for being down here in the first place. Then everyone would be down here, gawping. I wouldn't have the place to myself. People would forget who found it in the first place. This way, I could come down here whenever I wanted, with no one to disturb me, and get in and out of the city whenever I wanted. I could come here and think. *This place is special; no one but me even knows it's here — it's mine, no one else's, my own private place with better images than anywhere else in Trion!"*

Yes, Zeth thought, *that's exactly like Zia.* She was always a rebel and a loner; Albo was her only friend, if you could call him that, more like a younger brother.

"Do you think this was real or just someone's dream?" asked Zia.

"What do you mean?" asked Zeth.

"Well," she replied, "do you think this is how things were, many years ago, that Trion was really like this and the Lion-men were all cuddly and nice as they are here, or is this just someone's fantasy, just something made-up?"

Zeth looked at the images again. They were bursting with life and energy. Every figure, every creature, every blade of grass even, seemed to vibrate with life and with the love of life. It was wonderful.

"This isn't made-up," he replied. "It's a vision, and all visions are true."

"What do you mean?" asked Zia.

"Look at those stars," said Zeth. "We know they have been there for millions and millions of years and will still be there in millions of years when we have all gone. Think of all that time and space. Somewhere, sometime, this exists. Everything that is possible to be imagined, imagined clearly and strongly, is an image of truth, something that can be born out of time's vast womb and be 'real' in the way that you mean. It is an image-maker's task to show these things to us, and that's what these image-makers did, long ago."

Zia looked at him quizzically. "You're crazy," she said. "But talking about time, hadn't we better move on, before it gets too dark outside?" With that, she walked across the room and led Zeth towards the exit. It appeared to be simply a large black rock – part of the landscape around the river – but this was an illusion; the blackness was the beginning of the exit passage.

"You know the first time I came here," said Zia, "I missed this – I thought the passage just stopped at the chamber with no other exit! It was only on my second visit I discovered it was another way out."

As he was about to enter the passage, Zeth hesitated and looked back. He was afraid. Would he ever return to Trion? The enormity of what he was doing suddenly swept over him. He suddenly wanted to run back to the city, to tell Fidias about the chamber of images and then go home to his parents. What was he doing, taking this dreadful risk? He shook a little, hovering between the chamber and the passage leading out of Trion and into the lion's den. He so wanted to go back.

"Well?" said Zia, watching him, puzzled.

But then he rehearsed what going back would mean. He would not be going back to the Trion he knew and loved, to a safe city full of people he loved. That city was already gone. It was no longer safe, and many people he knew had already died. He remembered why he was doing this: because he was convinced that if he did nothing, the city would fall and everyone he loved, and he himself, would die. He sighed deeply, plucked up his courage, became resolute and followed Zia, wonderful, fearless Zia, into the passage.

As they walked, Zeth noticed that they were climbing – the floor had a gentle upwards gradient, taking them up towards ground level. After a few minutes, he could hear water ahead. Not the gentle flow of a river but the sound of very heavy rain – was it raining outside? The noise became louder and louder until it was clear that it could not be rain.

"What's that?" Zeth asked.

Zia smiled and said, "We're there." They turned an abrupt corner and indeed they were there, at the end of the passage facing a dead end: a solid stone wall with the noise of heavy rushing water coming from behind it.

Zia stepped aside and pointed to a large brass handle set into the stone. She smiled again – she was revelling in showing Zeth all the things she had discovered, known only to herself, her secret. She raised her torch and slipped it into a torch holder above head height. Zeth could see she had done this many times before.

"Put your torch out and leave it here," she ordered Zeth. "You won't need it now, but we will need it when we come back, if we come back."

Zeth obeyed her and watched as she seized the brass bar-shaped handle and pushed down using all her weight. There was a click and a thud from inside the stone wall. Then Zia pulled, walking backwards, legs bent low, as she slowly heaved the stone wall open. The noise of crashing water grew louder, and light streamed in from the setting sun.

It was a relief to breathe the fresh outside air. In front of them was a sheet of falling water – they were standing behind a waterfall.

Zeth stepped forward, screwing his eyes up as they adjusted to the bright light. He felt the spray from the falling water as he found himself on a narrow ledge behind the waterfall. He looked to the right and then to the left and realised immediately where he was. They were at the river where, in better times, he had often bathed. He had been here before, with many other children, having scrambled down the rocky bank and stood behind the waterfall cooling themselves in the spray on hot summer days, completely unaware that the rock face behind them was a door leading to a passage that went right into the heart of Trion. He saw immediately how clever this was. Anyone coming out of the door would be completely invisible – hidden behind the waterfall – keeping the existence of this other entry into the city hidden.

It all began to make some sense now to Zeth. It was vital to keep this entrance a secret, even from the citizens of Trion. Only a few people could ever have been allowed to know of its existence. At some point, this secret must have got lost to everyone – perhaps the last person to have knowledge of it had died before he or she could pass it on, and the secret was lost completely, until Zia, purely by accident, had chanced upon it. But, he mused, what had been its purpose? And why the chamber of images?

Zia pushed the door almost closed. She explained that she had never found a way to open it from the outside – maybe there wasn't one, she ventured. Usually, she closed it completely and returned via the normal entrance to the city.

They scrambled up the riverbank to the top of the waterfall. Zeth looked back at the city silhouetted against the setting sun. The other way lay the wood, with Agon's camp stretched out along the edge of it. Again, a wave of fear swept over him. But there was no turning back now – he took a deep breath and said, "Come on, let's go," and strode out across the plain towards the wood.

As they reached the edge of the wood, they had to make a decision: "Through the wood or round the edge – what do you think?" asked Zeth.

"We'll get closer before being spotted through the wood, but we want to be spotted, don't we?" replied Zia.

"Hmm… I think through the wood," said Zeth. "When we get caught, it's better if we aren't seen from Trion. I don't want my parents to know until they have to."

They entered the wood, and for the first time, Zeth noticed Zia looking worried. They walked slowly, looking nervously around them. They had not gone more than twenty paces when they were met by a wall of spears in front of them, the points only a hand's breadth from their chests.

Zia glanced behind – the same. They were surrounded, with no warning – they had not heard a thing. They froze and waited. Then the spears in front of them parted and a Lion-man stepped forward. He drew his sword. Zeth, fearing they were to be killed on the spot, said, "We have—" but before he could finish, the Lion-man held the sword pointed at his throat and said, "Silence!" He looked behind them and said, "Well?"

A voice replied, "There is no one else – they are alone. The plain is empty."

The Lion-man looked at them suspiciously and walked slowly around them, all the time keeping them at the point of his sword. One of the other Lion-men said, "What shall we do with them, Iordic?"

Iordic held up his hand to silence him, then said, "What are you doing here? Where did you think you were going?"

Zeth sighed with relief. At least he had a chance to speak, to explain. Now they had a chance.

"We have come to see Agon," he said nervously. "We have come to give him what he wants: the Lion-Image of Trion."

Iordic laughed and said, "What, you think you can just stroll over here and ask to see Agon? He will kill you! You expect us to believe that you – two children – have the Lion-Image?"

"But we do," said Zeth. "Here," and he reached into his shoulder bag.

"Wait!" ordered Iordic. He gingerly opened the bag with the point of his sword and peered in.

"Alright," he said. "Take it out."

Zeth took out the image and turned its face forwards towards Iordic. The Lion-men gasped and moved backwards. Iordic seemed transfixed for a moment, staring at the image. Zeth watched them. He recalled Fidias telling him that the Lion-men did not have image-makers and that they did not make images of any merit. They had heard descriptions of the Lion-Image and had tried to depict it, but their attempts were very crude and lacked any expression or feeling. Seeing this image must have amazed them – they had never seen anything like it before.

"You expect us to believe that this is the real Lion-Image? That Trion has sent this to us with two children! Why?"

"Trion did not send this to you," replied Zeth, growing more confident. "We stole it to bring it to Agon, to give him what he wants, to stop the killing."

Iordic looked at them curiously. There was something he admired about these children. He did not know what to believe, but here they were, in great danger, holding their nerve. He could hear the sincerity in Zeth's voice, and he could not help but like him and the girl, silent but smirking, fearless. What a strange pair.

One of his men said: "Iordic, this looks like the real thing. It makes me feel something, something strange. I think it's real, Iordic."

"You think it looks like the real thing? How can you know?" asked Iordic. "You have never seen the real thing!"

"I know, Iordic, but look – it has some strange power. I think we should take it to Agon. I fear it."

"Bind them together, and tether them," ordered Iordic. "We will take them to Agon to decide."

They were led through the camp, tethered like a pair of animals. All the Lion-men stood and turned to look at them in wonder, and a steady murmuring rippled around the camp. Soon they were being followed by a crowd of Lion-men curious to watch them and see what was happening. Zeth noticed many wounded scattered around the camp, and he thought he could see, over at the far edge of the camp, a heap of bodies. He noticed that the shelters these men had were crude and flimsy – conditions were not good.

Soon, however, they arrived at something much grander: a large, impressive tent with a canopied entrance, guarded by two Lion-men. In front of the entrance was a tall, sturdy wooden post. "Keep them by the whipping post," said Iordic and entered the tent. After a few minutes, he came out, took the tether and led them in.

Entering the tent was like crossing into another world. On one side was a huge four-poster bed covered with thick quilts. On the other sides were several oak tables laden with food, some half eaten. A large wrought-iron lantern hung from the centre of the vaulted ceiling; under it Agon was seated on a throne-like chair, one hand stroking the shaft of a double-headed axe leaning against his knee. The chair was set upon a high dais so that, although he was seated, he was looking down on anyone who came to see him. Either side of him were two armed guards. One a large man with, unusually for a Lion-man, a bald head. On the other side, dwarfing even the bald-headed man, stood Sogon, a mountain of muscle and armour, arms crossed. There were other Lion-men standing around the tent, only lightly armed and not armoured, unlike the guards. The whole scene was devised to intimidate, if not terrify.

Zeth felt the blood drain from him, and his breathing become shallow. He doubted, at that moment, that he would be able to speak. He observed Agon and noticed that he was stocky and muscular. But it was the head that was remarkable: a full head of golden hair, the face almost entirely hidden in a bristling golden beard, the eyes set so far into his head that you could barely see them – it would be easy to mistake this head for a lion's. No wonder they were called Lion-men, but Agon looked so much more like a lion than any of the others.

Agon observed them coldly, then smiled and said, "Iordic, please, make our guests more comfortable – remove the ropes from them. They can do us no harm, and I am sure they can see that escape is impossible. But then, they do not want to escape, do they? I believe they have come to speak to me." Iordic did as he was instructed and stood aside.

"So, children of Trion, tell me, what can I do for you?"

The words sounded so kind and civilised – they were 'guests' to be made 'comfortable', 'what could he do for them?'. But to Zeth, the words were terrifying. He was not fooled – he knew that Agon was playing with them. He was simply showing his complete control over them.

"Well?" asked Agon.

Zeth took a deep breath and found his voice: "We have come to give you what you want; we have come to give you the Lion-Image, to stop the bloodshed, so we can live in peace."

"Have you now?" said Agon. "Tell me, what is your name?"

"Zeth," he replied.

"Well, Zeth," he said, "it seems to me that you are not in a very good bargaining position. Assuming you have what you say in that little bag of yours, why don't I just take it and then attack the city that now no longer has the power of the Lion-Image to protect it?"

"Because," replied Zeth, "you would have what you came for. And even though the city would no longer have the Lion-Image, it still has many soldiers determined to defend it, and as well as the outer walls, you can see there are the inner walls around the Council Chamber that are heavily defended. Even if you take the city, you will lose many men – why would you do that if you have what you came for?" His voice shook as he spoke, but nevertheless he spoke clearly.

Iordic could not help but admire this boy. How well he spoke and under such pressure.

Agon nodded slowly, smiled and said, "So, Zeth, show me the image."

Zeth took the image out of his shoulder bag and did just as he did when showing it to Iordic – he turned it face forwards towards Agon so that he saw its most powerful aspect. A gasp came from all the Lion-men in the room – all except Agon, who simply looked coldly at it. If it evoked any feeling in him, he was careful not to show it. He rose from his chair, stepped down from the dais. "Here, set it here," ordered Agon, indicating the stump of a tree that served as a small table near the foot of the dais.

Zeth stepped forward and did as he was told. He noticed that Agon had brought the axe down from the dais with him. It was a terrifying observation – what did Agon intend to do with it? Zeth stepped back to Zia's side – he felt her presence comforting.

Agon tilted his head and looked at the Lion-Image and then walked slowly round it, observing it closely.

"And you," he said, holding the axe head under Zia's chin, "you, silent one, what is your name?"

She looked at him, smirking. "Zia," she said, without flinching, without a trace of fear in her voice.

Agon paused for a moment and looked at her curiously. Then he continued his walk around the image.

"Boric!" shouted Agon to one of the Lion-men in the tent. "What do you think of this? Is this the real Lion-Image or just a fake to trick us?"

Boric looked confused and frightened. It was clear he was terrified he might say the wrong thing.

"I, er… well… it seems like… it has some power, its eyes… well… I have never seen anything like this before —"

"Silence, fool!" shouted Agon.

Zeth watched Agon out of the corner of his eye. It was all he could do not to start shaking. He knew he had made a huge miscalculation. He had thought that Agon would be a normal man, someone you could reason with, someone who might take what he wants and then leave. He now saw that Agon was not like anyone else he had ever met. He felt the fear in the room – everyone was terrified of him. It was clear to Zeth that Agon was not interested in the Lion-Image; all he really wanted was power, power over everyone, and the key to his power was fear. He could see that Agon was calculating, calculating what to do, what would serve his crazy power lust most.

"So, Boric, you think this thing has power! Well, I will show you what I think!" Then he swung round, lifting the axe above his head and bringing it down with all his strength upon the image. It shattered into a thousand pieces. Fragments flew in every direction. Everyone turned away instinctively and covered their faces.

"You see!" shouted Agon in a fury. "Do you think that the real Lion-Image that has held the walls of Trion impregnable for all these years would shatter with one little tap from my axe?" He directed the question at Boric who was visibly shaking and mumbling, "N… no, Agon, I… I was mistaken; I do not have your wisdom, Agon."

Zeth began to understand what the 'whipping post'

might be for and shuddered at the thought of what it must be like serving Agon.

"It is a trick! Do they think I am a fool?! To send two children into my camp with this trinket and think that I would be stupid enough to be so easily deceived?"

He strode towards Zeth and Zia. Zeth was convinced he was about to kill them both immediately. But he didn't. "Well, children," he said, "I shall return you to the city, or at least part of you. Tomorrow, Iordic, you will send a messenger under a flag of truce to the city's gate. They will no doubt be expecting us to respond to their offer. The messenger will make them an offer – either they surrender in one hour, lay down their arms and open the gates, or I will send the head of one of these pretty little children flying over the walls to them. And if that does not persuade them, then the second head will follow at noon! Now take them away and bind them to the whipping post until dawn!"

Iordic seized their hands and took them outside. He sat them back to back against the whipping post and ordered two of his comrades to bind them to the post and to bind their hands and feet.

Zeth sat trance-like, completely dejected. He understood now what had happened to Zia after the death of Albo. He felt numb, dead inside. His plan had been a disaster. Trion would never throw down its arms to save him and Zia, but it was not his own death he feared – it was the unimaginable agony that it would bring upon his parents, especially the manner of his death. He was bereft of hope.

Iordic looked at them and felt a great sense of remorse. He almost regretted bringing them to Agon but knew there was nothing else he could do with so many others around. He knew that Trion would not surrender for two children, and he also knew that Agon knew this. It would just be a senseless execution of two children that would serve no purpose other than to satisfy Agon's cruelty. He almost felt angry at the children for being so stupid.

"Why did you come here?" he asked. "And how did they let you come here? Did you not realise it would be certain death, for nothing?" He said this to release his feeling of anger, sadness and frustration.

Zeth just stared; he could not speak. Zia looked at Iordic and said, "How could we know that your great leader was such a lying, raging animal? He is neither a lion nor a man nor any creature of any worth. You are all worthless savages!" Zia had more fight left in her than Zeth because she had already lost almost everything. She cared more about Zeth now than anyone, and her anger was for him and Albo, not for herself.

Iordic knelt beside them and said, "We are not all savages. We do not all agree with everything that Agon does."

"Then why," asked Zia, "did another of your kind kill a small boy running for safety? Your first act on coming here was to kill a small child. How I would like to kill that animal!"

"You don't need to," said Iordic. "He was a friend of mine; he is already dead."

"Then I hope it was a horrible, lingering death," said Zia.

"He took his own life," replied Iordic. "He fell upon his own sword. But before that he had fallen into darkness and lost the will to live. He fired an arrow at the walls, but it fell short. He could not get the death of the child out of his mind; he tortured himself, so your wish has been granted, and he was not a savage."

Zeth looked at Iordic. He saw the pain in his face and knew that he was quite different from Agon. *Not all Lion-*

men are savages, he thought. He recalled something that Fidias said: Not all arrows reach their intended targets. Maybe Fidias was right – maybe the Lion-men were not so different from the people of Trion, despite their appearance. He had never been so close to a Lion-man before, but now he could see how different they were from him, the skin so pale and almost red in places that you could see the blue veins underneath it. And the hair so straight and blond, so unlike the people of Trion with their smooth, almost black, skin and the tight, curly black hair. Listening to Iordic, he felt that he cared about them – the children of his enemies – and that Iordic was just as human as he and Zia.

"I will get you some food," said Iordic.

"Don't bother," said Zia. "Somehow I don't think we will feel much like eating."

***

Chiron was working late in the House of Healing. As the senior healer, he felt the burden of crisis caused by the fever weigh heavily upon his shoulders. He was looking at the meticulous records, made by his fellow healers, of all those stricken by the fever, looking for patterns, for signs that would help him stop or slow the spread of the disease and to shorten the recovery times of those who caught it. He knew that fighting the disease was just as important as fighting the Lion-men – in fact, unless they could stop the disease from spreading soon, there would not be enough citizens able to fight, and the city would fall. His work was, at this moment, more important than that of any one soldier, or even of the Captain of the Guard, in defending the city.

He analysed the situation logically. He could not stop the spread of the disease because he knew it was spread from person to person when they were close together. If one member of a family caught it, it spread quickly to the rest. Similarly, if one soldier in a band caught it then it quickly spread to their comrades in the same band. The obvious solution was to separate people, to keep them apart until the disease ran its course and passed. But in time of war, this was impossible – soldiers had to fight side by side. He decided, therefore, to focus on getting those who caught the disease better quickly, to find a way to make them recover in a few days rather than two weeks, which was the average time it took naturally.

Few people died of disease, but the high fever it caused, along with aching limbs and extreme lethargy, made it impossible for them to fight or indeed do anything other than lie in bed until they recovered. The healers had different ideas on how to cure it. Some said that the fever was good, that it was the body's way to fight the disease and should be left to run its course. Others maintained that the fever did great harm and caused the other symptoms and should be reduced by the administration of potions and the application of cooling cloths to the body to reduce it. Chiron had to decide which was right quickly and had decided to carry out a tryal, the way the citizens of Trion always decided the right course – 'Tryals not Arguments' were the words inscribed over the entrance to the House of Healing.

So, he was going through the records, finding the names of all those who had been brought in on the same day. He would divide them into two groups. One would have their fever reduced and the other would be left with a high fever, and this way he hoped to decide the best course. Then he would move on to other tryals, using different herbs and potions to judge their effects in the same way. The problem was, all this took time, and time was what he feared he did not have. He sighed heavily and wrote down instructions for the tryals to begin immediately in the morning.

He was about to leave when he heard footsteps entering the building. He stepped out of his room to find Fidias, the image-maker, and Tormon, the Captain of the Guard, coming towards him – *a very strange combination,* he thought, *and at this hour!*

"Good evening, Chiron," said Tormon. "We are looking for my son, Zeth – he is missing and we wondered if he might be visiting Zia who I believe is still here."

"Yes," replied Chiron. "She is doing well with her recovery and should be going home in a couple of days, but for the moment she is still here. I will take you to her room."

Tormon had been very worried when Zeth had not returned home that evening. At first, he was not too concerned – he thought he would find him in the House of Images. He was angry because the city was no longer safe at night now that Lion-men had started hiding within the city walls and attacking people after dark, and Zeth was under strict instructions to come home at dusk. So, he had set off, fully armed to bring him home. It was when he discovered he was not with Fidias that he began to worry.

"Maybe he is with Zia," suggested Fidias, even though he thought it unlikely – the healers would have told him to leave by now. Still, it was possible, so they both walked to the House of Healing to look for him.

"Chiron," said Tormon, "how is your work with the fever going? Do we have a cure yet or some way of shortening the illness?"

Chiron shook his head. "We are beginning tryals tomorrow, but this takes time, and I know time is what we do not have."

They looked in Zia's room, but it was empty. All three men stood looking at the empty room. Tormon felt deeply troubled; he felt crushed by the weight of office, the impossible task of defending the city with a rapidly shrinking army and now his own son missing.

"Wherever they are," said Fidias, "I will wager they are together."

"I will start a search," said Tormon, struggling to stop his voice from trembling. He turned on his heel and marched quickly away.

"Tormon!" shouted Fidias after him. "When you have organised the search, come to see me – I have an idea, but I need to go back to the House of Images; come to see me there."

"Why?" asked Tormon. "What are you thinking? Do you know where they are?"

"I need to check something. It is a mad idea; it is best I say nothing now, but please, come to see me when you have started the search."

Tormon frowned, but he had no time to argue, and he hurried on his way to give orders to all the soldiers on the night watch to start searching.

He roused twenty soldiers by the watchtower, divided them into pairs and ordered them to search every quarter of the city. He then went to the House of Images to see what Fidias had to say. He found Fidias seated, his arms folded, thinking. It occurred to him that it was the first time he had ever visited Fidias – always to get Zeth – and not found him working. "Well," he said, "what do you have to tell me?"

Fidias rose and drew back the curtain to reveal the Lion-Images. Tormon looked at them, perplexed. He picked one up and examined it. "You made these?" he asked.

Fidias nodded. "I showed them to Zeth a week ago. He was very worried – he had heard you talking about the fever and how it would lead to the fall of the city. He thought that Agon should be offered the Lion-Image to save the city. I showed him these and he left immediately."

"So…" said Tormon. "I don't understand."

"So now there is one missing, and so are Zeth and Zia."

"So, you think Zeth might have tried to take one to Agon!" exclaimed Tormon. "But that's impossible – he could never get out of the city; every inch of the walls is guarded day and night."

"And if you remember," said Fidias, "so they were on the first day of the siege, but somehow Zia got out with Albo. Shortly after Zeth left here, he managed to rouse Zia from her stupor and now they and one of my images are gone."

Tormon paced the room, agitated, lost for words. At last, he said, "But how can this be possible? Surely, he would not dare… how could they get out?"

"Your son is very strong-willed and brave," said Fidias. "Otherwise he would not keep coming here against your will and endure the mockery he does. When he is sure of the right course of action, he follows it no matter what. And Zia, she is a clever and resourceful girl and a rebel. The two of them together, well, anything is possible."

Tormon slumped down on a chair. "If this is true," he said, "then there is nothing… nothing we can do but wait. But I fear if they have gone to Agon's camp, they will never return. You must tell no one else about this. I cannot let Zeth's mother hear about it for now. I am going to the watchtower. Sleep is impossible. I will wait until dawn and search Agon's camp with the near-glass. There is nothing else I can do."

"I will come with you," said Fidias. "No man should face the night alone, nursing his worst fear."

***

Iordic lay in his tent. The sun had long since set, and the rise and fall of voices in the camp had ceased, but he could not sleep. He could not get the thought of the two children tied to the whipping post out of his mind. He knew their death would serve no purpose. The boy reminded him of his own son. And the girl – what courage. It was pointless to talk to Agon – to oppose him was fatal. He had to think of his own wife and son back home; he had to watch himself, please Agon and get home safely. That is what he told himself, over and over as the night slipped by, but in the end, he lost the argument with his conscience – he could not leave them to live through this desolate night, to face a grotesque death. He took his knife and slipped quietly out of his tent.

He looked carefully around the camp – everything was quiet; there was no sign of movement. He moved silently to the whipping post. As he approached, he could see the whites of Zia's eyes watching him. He held his fingers to his lips and shook his head slowly. He moved round her to face Zeth, who looked up sharply, aware of his presence – he made the same signal to him. Zeth saw the knife and thought for a moment that Iordic had come to kill them. Instead, he felt his bonds being cut. Iordic signalled silence again to reinforce the message. He then picked up the cut lengths of rope and put them into Zeth's shoulder bag – he did not want the cut ropes to be left as witness. He touched both their shoulders to ensure he had their attention and stretched out his arm, his palm flat and vertical, pointing down the side of Agon's pavilion towards Trion. He pointed to the left of this line and shook his head, and then to the right and did the same. Zeth and Zia both nodded; they understood – they were to go in that direction and no other.

Then, without another sign or gesture, he was gone – he had done what he could; it was now up to them.

It was fortunate that Agon did not allow anyone to bed down close to his quarters – he did not want the sound of snoring men to disturb him or anyone to eavesdrop on his conversations. So Zeth and Zia had a direct route out of the camp and onto the plain without risking disturbing any sleeping Lion-men on their way. Soon they were clear of the camp and onto the plain. It was a black, moonless night and they stumbled several times, each time fearing they would be heard by the Lion-men and snatched back again. They turned towards the river and soon the noise of the waterfall guided them back to the hidden door and the torches that would light their way back to Trion.

Chapter Thirteen

The Dreamer Meets
the Warrior

Zeth sat at the table. His father sat opposite him. His mother paced the room furiously. Zeth had told them everything, every detail.

"You are lucky to be alive!" she shouted. "How could you do such a thing without telling us?"

His father was oddly calm.

"You would not have let me go, and you would have been right," said Zeth. "But I thought it was the only chance we had to save the city, to save you, to save everyone. I was wrong."

"What he did, Lelka," said Tormon, "was very brave. We are lucky to still have him, and what he has discovered in Agon's camp may help us. And the secret way out of the city – that could be invaluable."

"I cannot understand why you are not angry," said Lelka. "You talk as though you approve of what he did!"

"I don't approve of what he did, but I understand why he did it, and I admire his courage. He tried to do what his father has failed to do, to save the city." Tormon wept, worn out by his great burden – the near loss of his son was the final straw. Zeth reached out and touched his arm, and for an instant the child was father to the man. Lelka came to them, her anger gone, and all three held each other, their faces wet with tears.

At last, Lelka said, "What are we to do? Do we have any hope of defeating this monster Agon?"

Tormon recovered and felt stronger. "I will go to see Thea now. I will ask her to summon the council and deliberate on all that Zeth and Zia have discovered."

***

As Tormon walked across to Thea's quarters by the Council Chamber, he came across some of the men he had sent to search for Zeth. He suddenly realised that he had forgotten to call off the search. He called them over and saw immediately that they looked exhausted, and one had blood on his sword. "We have found Zeth so, please, spread the word to call off the search. But what has happened?" he said, pointing to the sword.

"During the search," replied the man with the bloody sword, "we came across three Lion-men, hiding in the stables. They must have been part of the group that managed to break through during the last attack. We thought we had hunted them all down, but it seems we did not. We lost a man before we overwhelmed them. This is what we found on them." He gave Tormon a small bag.

Tormon looked in the bag and saw two severed ears – ears clearly of his own people. He drew back in disgust.

"We kept one of them alive," continued the soldier, "and promised to spare him if he told us the meaning of this. He told us that Agon had offered a reward for every ear they took back. He told us that Agon wanted as many Lion-men as possible to hide in the city and to strike in the night to spread terror amongst us, to deprive us of rest. Each ear was worth a lot to them. They planned to try to escape over the walls tonight. There seem to be more and more of them hiding around the city."

"I see," said Tormon and hastened to see Thea.

Although it was not quite dawn, he found Thea already at work at her desk. How she had aged since the siege began, her hair now almost all grey, her face lined and drawn. She stood and moved over to a more comfortable seat and invited Tormon to sit opposite her.

"Well, Tormon," she said, "it must be urgent for you to visit me at this hour." She listened in astonishment as Tormon related what Zia and Zeth had done. When he had finished, she asked:

"And where are Zia and Zeth now?"

"Zeth is at home sleeping. We have not even seen Zia. She was so exhausted she returned to her room in the House of Healing to sleep. Zeth says she has not yet fully recovered from her illness. She stayed strong until they were safe, but on returning to the city, she was close to collapse. We asked the healers to attend her while she slept."

"They were so lucky to find compassion in the camp of our enemies, but it seems we can expect no mercy from Agon if he overcomes us."

"I fear the worst, Thea. I do not know how much longer I can hold them at bay. No one is safe, even within the city walls. Even tonight, the night watch found three Lion-men hiding in the city, picking off easy victims. I have failed –

even my own son feels he has to try to end the siege on his own.”

“You have not failed,” said Thea. “The city would have fallen long ago but for you. Every decision you have made has been the right one. You have marshalled our forces brilliantly, and if it were not for this fever, I have no doubt you would hold the city until next winter and force Agon and his forces to leave.”

“But we have the fever,” said Tormon. “And I don’t know how much longer we can avoid being overrun.”

“This burden is not yours alone,” replied Thea, placing her hand on his. “We must call a council meeting. The discovery of a secret way out of the city is important, as is the fact that Agon does not have the full support of all his troops. There is much we can explore. But before we call a meeting, I want to visit Chiron and see how things are with the sick and the search for a cure. I also want to let all the councillors know what has happened, so they have time to deliberate and come up with some ideas before the meeting. How long do you think we have, Tormon, before the situation is hopeless?”

“Unless there is a miracle in the House of Healing,” replied Tormon, “maybe two weeks at most.”

“I shall call a meeting in two days,” said Thea. “Now you should go and sleep. This must have been the worst of nights for you.”

As he left Thea’s quarters, light was already in the sky. He had thought that Thea would call an emergency meeting of the council the same day and was worried that much valuable time could be lost by waiting two days. Reflecting on the meeting, he suddenly realised how tired and drawn Thea looked. Maybe she had not slept; maybe she could not face a meeting that day. He knew that the recent death of her brother in battle had affected her profoundly – could she be reaching breaking point? But then, maybe she was right – the councillors needed time to consider what had happened before coming together immediately to make the most important decisions they would ever have to make.

He headed home, downcast and worried, but he knew much of it was tiredness. He needed a few hours' sleep to revive his spirits and prepare him to face what lay ahead. He was fortunate that Agon did not order an attack that day – he was too busy raging at the escape of Zeth and Zia and investigating how it could have happened.

***

Tormon awoke just after midday. He was relieved to find Zeth still sleeping in his room. He washed, ate, put on his armour and went out to see what was happening. First, to the walls to see if there was any activity in Agon's camp. The morning, it seemed, had been quiet, but now there was lots of activity around the siege engines – it looked like Agon was preparing for another major attack upon the city, but not imminently. Then to the House of Healing to see if there were any developments there. Chiron told him that Thea had been there earlier, and he could only tell Tormon what he had told her, that more people had been admitted that day than had been released – the numbers affected by the fever were still growing; in fact, they seem to be accelerating. Although Chiron was not a councillor, Tormon asked him to attend the meeting when it was called – the situation in the House of Healing would be critical to any decisions made; they would need him there. "Yes," said Chiron. Thea had already invited him.

Tormon then went to see Zia. She was awake, sitting on her bed stroking the rabbit. She looked startled and worried when she saw Tormon, no doubt expecting a reprimand for what she had done. She was surprised when instead Tormon said, "Thank you, Zia, for going with Zeth. It would have been even more terrible for him alone. You are a brave girl. We may need to speak to you soon. Thank you." He then just turned and left, leaving her open-mouthed in astonishment.

Now to go underground to the secret passage. He needed to see for himself the size and length of it. But he did not want to go alone – he wanted another pair of eyes, and who better than Fidias? Maybe he could also explain the strange chamber of images that Zeth had described to him. He found Fidias working as usual – nothing seemed to stop the image-maker from creating his strange images. Tormon quickly told Fidias what he had learnt from Zeth and asked if he would accompany him to the chamber of images. Fidias readily agreed – he was intrigued.

As they walked across the city to the entrance to the subterranean river, Tormon asked, "How could it be that there is such a thing under the city and yet nobody knew about it? We have plans in the Houses of Learning of every building in the city and of every building that has ever existed – how could such a thing remain secret?"

"But clearly," replied Fidias, "it was meant to be secret – no one builds a secret exit from a place and then leaves plans around for anyone to see. Also, to keep it a secret, only a few people would have known about it, and maybe all those who knew simply died without passing the knowledge on, or those to whom it was passed onto died unexpectedly, leaving the knowledge of it lost. But not entirely – I have heard rumours of a secret underground exit from the city, and the obvious location is where we are going now. But it seems to have been so cleverly concealed that even after many years of maintaining and examining the river passage, it was never discovered. I never gave any credence to such rumours because almost every walled city and ancient fortified building that has ever existed has such rumours about it."

"And it took a clever girl like Zia to find it, after all this time," said Tormon.

"Yes," said Fidias. "Thank goodness for the rebels amongst us. Those who are different, like Zia and Zeth."

He did not mention himself, but Tormon caught his drift.

Tormon had come to like and respect Fidias. Formerly, he had held him in disdain, but his skill and bravery in battle, and his companionship and thoughtfulness during his long, anxious night, had warmed Tormon towards him.

Zeth had told his father precisely which torch holder to pull to open the secret door. They were quickly into the passage and down to the chamber of images. Fidias, like Zeth, was amazed at the quality and condition of the images. He gazed upon them lovingly and looked set to spend hours there examining every inch of the chamber.

"Fidias," said Tormon, "you can come back here now whenever you like and spend as long as you like. But now we must go and see the rest of the passage and the exit. I counted fifty-two paces from the start of the passage to the chamber, and the entrance to the river itself is close to the east wall, so I reckon that we are already outside the city walls here. We must now pace the distance to the exit."

Fidias smiled and said, "Forever the practical man – even in the midst of all this beauty, you have diligently paced out the distance to here. How a city needs people like you and me – so different yet both so necessary."

"Yes, but we must go," said Tormon.

Fidias laughed. "Now I know where Zeth gets his persistence from."

They left the chamber and Fidias paced the distance to the exit: a much longer distance of six hundred and fifty paces, but even so, only a few minutes. Tormon was astonished. "How many times have I stood behind this waterfall as a boy," he said, "and not known that there was a secret entrance to the city right behind me?!"

They returned to the chamber and, once again, Tormon had to practically drag Fidias out of it.

"Can't you leave me here and return on your own?" asked Fidias.

"No," replied Tormon.

"Why not?" asked Fidias.

"Because I'm frightened of the dark," joked Tormon.

It was not entirely a joke. Tormon was frightened of the darkness in his soul. He was deeply troubled and wanted Fidias's company. "I feel we are reaching the end game," he said, "and I fear it will not end well."

"I fear it too," said Fidias. "Zeth has had this fear from the beginning, from the first blowing of the horn. He truly has vision, an instinctive foresight of what may come to pass. Sometimes, this vision is mistaken for cowardice. But often such people are the bravest – they have more practice at overcoming fear. Zeth certainly had to overcome great fear last night."

"The council is to meet soon – can you come?"

"But I am not a councillor," said Fidias. "And what could they possibly learn from an image-maker whom they despise."

"I think we may have despised image-making for too long," said Tormon. "And I may need you to speak about

Zeth. Chiron is not on the council either, but he is to come too – we will need everyone who has something to offer at this meeting; it may be our last."

"Of course, I will come."

***

Agon was raging after the escape of Zia and Zeth. The whole episode had unsettled him. He could not understand it. Was some magic involved? Two children appeared out of nowhere at the edge of his camp bearing what they claimed to be the Lion-Image. He had found the image strangely unsettling, but he could not allow anyone to think that it really was the Lion-Image. He knew that many of his soldiers were weary of the siege and wanted to return home, and he did not want them to have any excuse. He wanted to take the city at any cost and make Trion the seat of his own personal empire, so he had smashed the image to pieces. *How*, he wondered, *had these children escaped without trace?* Even the ropes which bound them had gone.

He entertained the thought for a while that it was a traitor – someone within his own camp perhaps – but why? Why should anybody take that risk? They knew that he would torture and kill them if they were discovered, and they had nothing to gain. Because he had no compassion, he could not understand how it might motivate others. It was inconceivable to him that someone might risk their life for others – others whom they did not even know; others who were not even their kinsmen. Maybe they had help from Trion. Maybe there were others around watching, who crept into the camp to release them – in which case his men were to blame for incompetence and stupidity. So, he raged for hours, shouting at everyone who had found the children and those who had tied them – in fact, anyone who came anywhere near him.

Iordic feared that he might be slain anyway, even though Agon did not suspect him of treachery. But in the end the storm passed, and Agon decided that he would redouble his attack on the city. Maybe the city was on the verge of surrender or collapse. Maybe this ruse with the children was a last desperate throw of the dice. Now was maybe the time to strike hard. So, he ordered that the siege engines be prepared and weapons be readied for an attack on three different sections of the walls, to split the defence and probe for weaknesses. Sogon, too, was to be brought into play after the initial attack had been launched, to maximise the impact and to spread fear and panic, as he always did.

Tormon, of course, knew that the attack was coming. He visited all the troops, gauging their preparedness and making sure they all knew what was expected of them. He doubled the night guard just in case Agon launched a night attack – it would not be the first time, but Agon preferred to attack in the early morning from the east, with the sun at his back, blinding the eyes of the defenders. When he had done all he could, he returned home to be with his family, more aware than ever that every night with them might be his last.

***

The attack commenced as usual with an assault on the walls just to the east of the main gate. The idea was to get as many men over the wall as close to the gate as possible so that they could attempt to open it from the inside. However, Tormon had long since stationed a permanent force behind a makeshift wall surrounding the gate to protect it. In the past, it had acted almost like a magnet for those few Lion-men who made it past the wall's defences, and they could be dealt with there swiftly. But more recently, Agon had adopted a different tactic. Knowing that the gate was heavily defended on the inside, he had instructed his men to hide themselves throughout the city and cause havoc at night. This was much more difficult to deal with. Tormon now had a sizeable force at the gate doing nothing – the mere threat of an attack on the gate kept them there but rendered them inactive, and now that so many of Tormon's soldiers were laid low by the fever, it was a force that Tormon could ill afford to spare doing nothing. Still, he had enough soldiers to hold the first attack and the second, which was launched at the north side of the city and was to be expected. It was when the third attack came to the south-west that Tormon really began to worry. It was clear that Agon was holding nothing back this time – he was throwing everything at them to try to overwhelm them.

Tormon was at the top of the watchtower with his near-glass, directing operations. He signalled his instructions to his reserve force below, and to his commanders on the walls, using a mirror. When the sun did not shine, he had to use runners. As he dispatched the last of his soldiers to the south-west, he realised that for the first time, he had little left in reserve. If one section of the wall were overwhelmed, he would have no option but to weaken the forces by the gate, which would be very risky. Over three hundred soldiers were now sick in the House of Healing and many more were sick in their homes – if only he had them now!

Han stood at the foot of the steps up to the wall in the south-west, despatched there along with four spearmen to deal with any Lion-men that made it past the first line of defence. As usual, he carried his heavy, double-handed mace. He was not agile enough to use a sword and shield, but he was very strong, and one swing of his mace, if it hit its target, would fell any enemy. He could see that they were struggling on the wall and grew impatient. At last, he could wait no longer and hobbled up the steps. "Han," shouted one of his companions, "you are to wait here!" Han merely scowled back and ignored him. He approached the top of the steps where a furious battle was taking place. He was just in reach of the legs of a Lion-man. He leaned against the wall, braced himself and swung his mace, breaking the attacker's leg – he tumbled from the wall to be despatched by Han's companions below. Han now hauled himself up another step to bring himself within reach of another pair of legs and repeated the same again. "This is child's play," he shouted to the spearmen below. "One tap of my little stick and they tumble like puppets!"

"Look out!" shouted all the spearmen in chorus.

As Han turned to look up, he was bowled over by two soldiers tumbling down the steps. All three ended in a heap at the bottom of the steps, one dead, one wounded and Han cursing and struggling to get to his feet. He noticed that all the spearmen were retreating fearfully, in formation, spears held in front of them. Han turned and saw Sogon and his escort at the top of the steps – he had scythed through the defenders on the wall as though they were a field of corn. Han scowled, readying his mace, and shouted, "Come on, you great beast!"

Sogon came down the steps, his escort in close attendance. Han limped forward and swung his mace. Sogon stepped aside and proffered his shield. It was only dealt a glancing blow, but even so, Sogon was surprised by the weight of it – his shield suffered a deep dent and his arm felt numb for an instant. He raised his sword and made to step forward. The spearmen advanced to support Han.

Then one of Sogon's escorts shouted, "Sogon, remember our orders," and nodded in the direction of the centre of the city. Sogon glared at Han, then all three ran away from the walls and into the city. Meanwhile, more Lion-men began to pour down the steps through the breach created by Sogon. Han and the spearmen hesitated, wondering for a moment what they should do, but then, judging that the wall was their priority, they advanced to the steps and started to spear the Lion-men before they reached the bottom of the steps. They were soon joined by reinforcements, forming a forest of spears around the base of the steps.

Tormon had observed everything from the watchtower. He saw the approach of Sogon even before the defenders on the wall and had already signalled to deploy troops from the gate defences. Now he was deeply worried – Sogon was heading into the city, and he had lost track of him; the gate's defences were weakened, and the three battles on the walls were still in the balance. All he had left was fifty men at the base of the watchtower. He handed the near-glass to Yan, who had almost become his permanent assistant. "Here," he said, "try to find Sogon and follow his movements – use the mirror to signal me if you find him; keep track of him whatever you do." He then took twenty men with him and led them up onto the walls to try to swing the battle his way. He knew that this was going to be a close thing.

Tormon cantered along the walls to the south-west, followed by his men. As he approached the section under attack, he leapt onto the parapet, then jumped across onto the siege engine's platform, sending two Lion-men flying off and down into the ditch below. He beckoned two of his men to do likewise. Now they were behind the Lion-men on the wall, who were exchanging blows with the defenders at the top of the steps, trying to drive them back. Surrounded, the Lion-men were soon dispatched. He then turned to the stream of attackers making their way up the inside of the siege engine. He told his men to hold them back then yelled below, "Han, get your backside up here with that mace of yours!"

Han made his way up the steps. "Now then," ordered Tormon, "smash this thing to bits, will you?"

"With pleasure," said Han.

A few swings of the mace against the timbers soon sent the top of the engine tumbling down to the ground, rendering the whole structure useless.

Further along the wall, there were numerous ladders being scaled by Lion-men. This battle had a long way to go yet, but Tormon's intervention had swung it the defenders' way. "Now finish the job!" he shouted to all the soldiers along the wall. "Come," he shouted to the men with him and ran down the steps and across the city to the battle in the east.

***

As the sun began to set, Tormon leaned against the bottom of the watchtower, the day's battle almost won. The last remnants of the siege engines and ladders were being smashed down from the walls, and the Lion-men were retreating to their camp. He was exhausted, but he had to find out where Sogon was. He called up to Yan, not wanting to scale the tower. "Sogon?" he asked.

"He was last seen in the market area," replied Yan.

Tormon gathered up the troops no longer needed on the walls and used half of them to seal off the market area and told the rest of them to get some sleep and relieve the others in six hours. He wanted to keep Sogon boxed in. This was going to be a long night, and in the morning was the council meeting, assuming Agon did not launch another attack.

He walked wearily home to see if Lelka had returned and take a brief rest. He was almost there when Yan came running, breathless. "Sogon is in the Houses of Learning," he gasped.

"How?" said Tormon. "You said he was in the market area."

"That's where I last spotted him," said Yan. "But as you know, it is a rabbit warren of huts, buildings and alleyways, and it is impossible to keep track of someone once they go in there. Somehow, he must have slipped out and made his way—"

"Yes, yes," interrupted Tormon. "Go over to the market area and get thirty spearmen and bring them over to the Houses of Learning and meet me there as quickly as possible. Go!"

Tormon slipped into his house to pick up a spear and called to Lelka. "Yes, I am here and alive!" she shouted.

"Where is Zeth?" he asked.

"He went to see Fidias," she replied.

Without another word, he picked up his spear and raced to the House of Images.

***

Zeth knew something was wrong as he approached the House of Images. The door was left open, and Fidias never left the door open. He recollected how, many years ago, when he entered the house for the first time, Fidias had scolded him for leaving the door open: "Shut the door, you fool! One puff of wind and years of work scattered everywhere!" He remembered how terrified he was. It seemed to have happened an eternity ago in a different world.

He stepped gingerly through the door and looked around. At first, all seemed in order – just an open door and no Fidias. Then his heart stopped as he saw a hand grasping a piece of charcoal on the floor, sticking out from behind the large table in the centre of the room. He forgot his fear and rushed round the table. Fidias lay on the floor, a gaping wound in his back, the charcoal in his right hand, a large parchment crumpled between his left arm and his body. He had almost certainly not even seen his attacker – he died as he had lived, lost deep in his images, working.

Zeth knelt by Fidias's body; he could scarcely breathe. By the hand with the charcoal was the word 'Zeth' and the symbol of the image-maker, the lion, perfectly drawn. Even when dying, Fidias had created a perfect image.

The clang of metal on stone made Zeth look up. In the doorway of the inner room stood Sogon, his head bent forward into the room, unable to fit under the doorway. He looked at Zeth and smiled, recognising him. Zeth froze. A spear flew over Zeth's head. Sogon only just lifted his shield in time. The spear deflected off it and clattered to the floor by Zeth.

Tormon stood in the open doorway. He had tried to catch Sogon off guard in the instant he saw him but failed. He launched himself at Sogon and swung his sword at his head. Sogon swatted it away with his shield, raised his leg and kicked Tormon's shield, sending him backwards into the wall. Tormon put his foot to the wall and launched himself forward again. He feinted another blow at Sogon's head but brought his sword down low and managed to catch the edge of his foot. Sogon roared with pain and brought his enormous sword down on Tormon, furiously striking his shield three times. The shield disintegrated. He kicked Tormon again, sending him back against the wall, the breath knocked out of him.

Tormon tossed the remains of his shield on his arm aside. There was nothing between him and this colossus now but his sword. He took his sword in both hands and hurled himself at Sogon, using every ounce of his weight and strength to drive the point through Sogon's shield at the only weakness he could see: the dent that Han's mace had made earlier, stretching the metal a little thinner. He felt the blade pass through, but only as far as Sogon's armour. Sogon twisted his shield, twisting Tormon's arm with it. The blade was now trapped by the shield; Sogon wrenched the sword from Tormon's hand and threw both shield and sword aside. He kicked Tormon again, full in the chest, sending him crashing into the wall, leaving him sitting on the floor, defenceless. Sogon stepped forward, raising his enormous sword, ready to strike the fatal blow.

Zeth could not remember picking up the spear, nor finding that perfect centre of balance on the shaft as he had been taught many times. Under Sogon's raised arm, Zeth saw a large area of exposed flesh, between his cuirass and his shoulder armour. He stepped forward, launching the spear, making sure that his arm followed through towards the target even after the spear had left his hand.

The spear passed right through Sogon's chest. His right arm that, an instant before, was a terrifying instrument of death, now fell limply onto the spear shaft and hung there. His eyes bulged. He tried to turn his head towards Zeth, but he could not. He swayed like a giant, helpless scarecrow in the wind, then fell, crashing to the ground, a great heap of armour and flesh.

Tormon leapt to his feet and extracted his sword from Sogon's shield. He was still anxious – where were Sogon's escorts?

He strode across the room and took Zeth's arm to lead

him out through the door, but Zeth tore himself away and fell upon Fidias's body, weeping. He took the charcoal from his master's lifeless hand and put it in his pocket. Tormon allowed him a few seconds of grief, looking around anxiously, then he said, "Come, Zeth, we must go."

Zeth pointed to his name and the image on the floor and said, "Look, what does this mean?"

"It means," replied Tormon, "that you are now the image-maker of Trion."

Chapter Fourteen

Council of Despair

Thea rapped her staff of office three times on the table and began: "Citizens of Trion, we meet in the darkest of times. Yesterday we repulsed another attack – Sogon was slain, but it was a hollow victory. Tormon, please…"

Tormon took a deep breath and began: "We were almost overrun. We were stretched to the limit and had we had fifty fewer soldiers, we would have been overrun. Well, now we have not fifty fewer soldiers but more than three hundred fewer. We lost nearly two hundred in the battle and the rest to the fever by this morning. If Agon attacks us again as he did yesterday – in three places simultaneously – we cannot hold them; the city will fall." He stopped speaking, and a stunned silence fell upon the Council Chamber.

At last, someone spoke: "But surely, Tormon, Agon has lost more fighters than we have – how would he be able to launch a similar attack again?"

"Yes," replied Tormon. "He lost over five hundred, and he lost Sogon. But this morning he received reinforcements

– more than six hundred Lion-men arrived in his camp. No doubt many that were here before and are now rested. For Agon, it is as though he lost no fighters. Even so, if we did not have hundreds laid low by the fever, we could still hold the walls, but we do, and we can't."

"Chiron," said another, "have we made no progress in curing this disease? This is what's killing us as much as Agon."

"No," replied Chiron. "It is too early yet. This is a new disease, and we have not had long enough to do sufficient tryals."

"You are moving too slowly," said another councillor. "We are at war, and you are proceeding at the same pace as normal, as though you have all the time in the world. All you know is that your first tryal was an error and told you nothing! You are carrying out one tryal at a time when you should be doing many!"

Chiron sighed and said, "You should have spent more time in the Houses of Learning, my friend. Many tryals at the same time would simply lead to confusion. And as those who have spent years seeking knowledge well know, knowledge is found more easily from error than from confusion."

"Enough!" said Thea. "We are where we are. The sick are sick, and there is nothing that can be done about that."

Then Han asked, "Chiron, why is it that the Lion-men are not afflicted by this disease? We know that it spreads quickly from one person to another, yet we are in close combat with the Lion-men, and it seems they are not stricken – why?"

"Because, Han," replied Chiron, "when you get close to Lion-men, you kill them, and they cannot spread the disease back in their camp!"

"Hmmm," muttered Han. "Maybe we should kiss them instead!"

Despite the gloom, a small ripple of laughter ran through the chamber.

"Hypasia," asked a councillor, "is Tormon correct? Are the numbers correct?"

"I am afraid he is," she replied. "I have counted the numbers slain and wounded on each side after every battle, and the ratios are similar each time. The fever has tilted the balance in the attackers' favour. We cannot hold back another attack like the last one – one section will fail and then the others will be overrun, and as Tormon has explained, we have no reserve force to stop them."

Again, a stunned silence.

"So, what are we to do?" asked Han. "Sue for peace? Try to strike a deal with Agon before he realises how desperate our situation is?"

"Before this meeting," replied Thea, "I spoke with Zeth at length. He thinks that Agon is ruthless and wicked; there is no negotiating with him. He wishes only to destroy us. I have to say that I believe he is right. Zeth seems to be an exceptionally perceptive child, and his judgement I am sure is good."

Silence.

"Are there no good options then?" asked another councillor. "Are we all simply to die in the next attack?"

"And the secret exit from the city?" asked another councillor. "Can this not be an escape route for us?"

Thea said, "Hypasia, please explain."

"Given the length and width of the passage as measured by Tormon," explained Hypasia, "it is not possible to evacuate the city before the next attack and without being seen. We would have to leave at night and get across the plain and into the woods at the foothills of the mountains without being spotted by the Lion-men. It is impossible – there are too many of us. I can go through the numbers if you like…"

"No, no," replied the councillor. "I am sure you are right."

Silence.

"Then what is to be done?" said another voice, trembling, sounding tired and desperate.

Thea replied, "Councillors, I fear that what I must say will offer you little comfort. There is no good choice. All paths now are bad. I can only offer you the least bad option. We have failed. The city will fall. But the discovery of the secret exit means that we can save most of our children." She paused; every head turned to her. There was absolute silence as she continued.

"All those children who can walk well can be saved. They must leave the city at dusk and walk across the plain to the mountains during the night. Meanwhile, we must abandon the walls and retreat into the Council Chamber buildings and the Houses of Learning. These walls, and the city walls behind them, form a natural citadel that can be defended for a while – for long enough to allow the children to escape. It will take them one night's walk to reach the trees at the beginning of the foothills. They must stay there during the day, hidden from view, while we keep Agon's attention on us here. One more night and they should be into the foothills and out of sight from the plain or even the highest building in the city, which by then may have fallen to Agon." She stopped speaking.

Tormon was shocked. He had not expected this. He had not known what to expect. He knew the situation was desperate and could not see a way forward. But this solution was totally unexpected. His head was spinning – the thought of watching Zeth leave the city and never seeing him again… and Lelka… could she bear it?"

As if to echo his thoughts, a councillor said: "Are you asking me to say goodbye to my child and to deprive him of his parents?"

"It is not my decision," replied Thea. "As you know, this must be a decision taken by all of us. And of course, we must consider alternatives – if there are any. But I am asking you to decide whether you would prefer your child to die here with you or be given a chance, a chance to live and start a new life, unless there is a better way…"

Tormon suddenly saw things clearly. He had always admired Thea, but he admired her now even more. She looked completely drained and yet she had thought things through so well, and it seemed to him that this was the only way to salvage something from the impending defeat, to save the children. His eyes drifted to the Lion-Image as they had on the first day of the siege, after the blowing of the horn. It now seemed like a rebuke. He felt the power of the image now, not as a guarantee of safety through some magical power but as a reminder, which they had long ignored, of the power of the imagination on which the city had been founded.

Stirred to speak, he said, "I fear Thea is right. Withdrawal to these buildings is our only chance to hold Agon at bay. We can save our children, and if by some miracle, we survive, we can be united with them again. This seems to be the only way to save what is most precious to us."

"But where will they go?" asked Han.

"Over the mountains," replied Thea. "To the land of the Kusai people. They are a gentle, peace-loving people. They hold no land but wander freely, herding their cattle. Your leather belt, Han, as you know, came from them. I am sure they would welcome our children and do them no harm."

"Or enslave them and turn them into herders," said a dissenting voice.

Thea spread her arms and said, "Please, give me an alternative."

Silence.

"If this is what we must do," said Han, "when must they go?"

"Tonight," said Tormon. "It has to be tonight. Agon could attack again as early as tomorrow."

"Can it be done?" asked Han. "Can we prepare the children to leave, get them out of the city and get the rest of the population out of their homes within this citadel in one day?"

"Yes," said Hypasia, who had been calculating furiously during the discussion. "It would take only three hours for all the children to walk out of the city and another four for them to walk across the plain and into the woods near the hills – it could all be done before dawn. There is enough room for the whole population to stay within these walls, but we must make haste and bring all the food and arms here quickly. We will still have access to two wells – we could withstand another siege here for some time."

"What do I tell my children?" asked another councillor. "How can I persuade them to leave their parents and the city?"

"You must tell them," said Thea, "that they are merely going ahead of you, so as not to slow the exit down. You must tell them that you will join them shortly, that it will only be a couple of days."

"You want me to lie to them, to make the last words I utter to my children a lie?"

"It will be a good lie," replied Han. "It will be a lie to save their lives. There are times when a lie is better than the truth. I remember Fidias, bless his soul, once saying that there are kind lies and harsh truths."

"I presume the children will need an armed escort. Some adults to lead them to safety," said a councillor.

Tormon shook his head. "There is no point," he said. "If they are discovered out in the open, they would be overwhelmed, even if all our forces went with them. No, we need every person capable of fighting here to slow down the fall of the city and buy them time. Time and distance are the only soldiers that can save them."

"Then who will lead them?" asked Han.

"It is clear who should lead them," replied Thea. "It must be Zeth and Zia. Since he slew Sogon, Zeth has become a hero overnight. All the children will follow him without question. What Zeth and Zia did in going to Agon was rash, but it showed great courage and resourcefulness. They know the way out; they know how to avoid wandering towards Agon's camp; and together they are strong."

"Hmm," muttered a councillor. "The dreamer has become a warrior – perhaps with one lucky throw."

Han snarled and replied angrily, "One lucky throw! I have seen hardened soldiers freeze at the sight of Sogon, unable to raise their sword or stand their ground. Zeth showed the same courage he displayed when venturing into Agon's camp. And what a throw, hitting the only gap in Sogon's armour perfectly. Two finger's width either side and the spear may well have glanced off Sogon's armour. I helped haul Sogon's body out of the House of Images and saw it with my own eyes. No, what Zeth did owed nothing to luck and everything to courage and skill!"

There was a murmur of assent around the table.

"So, Tormon," said Thea, "it seems your son is no longer a dreamer and has become a fine soldier after all, despite all the time he spent with Fidias."

"No," said Tormon. "He has become a leader, an image-maker in the line of Los who founded this city. And that is because of the time he spent with Fidias, not despite it – I see that now. I think we have ignored the art of image-making too long and have forgotten the ideals of Los which can be clearly seen in the chamber of images buried within the heart of the city, for those who would care to look."

There was silence, until Thea spoke for the last time: "So, Councillors, shall we vote on this plan, or is there another?"

They voted, and Thea's plan was carried. Many councillors wept as they raised their hands.

***

Zeth was called into the courtyard by Tormon and Lelka. The house had been emptied of anything that might be of use to the Lion-men: food, weapons, clothing. Even Lelka's archery target had disappeared from the courtyard. The house now seemed soulless. He knew that the plan was now to fall back into the council buildings and the Houses of Learning and had spent all day helping his parents move things from the house. He had a feeling of increasing unease, understandable given what was happening. But he sensed that something else was afoot he had not yet been told, and he was bracing himself for more bad news.

As he entered the courtyard, his father passed him a backpack. "Here," he said, "there is enough food in there for three days, a near-glass, a timekeeper, a pole-finder, a map and other things that you will need. And you should put on your sword that was to be given on your fourteenth birthday – you may have it early – and hopefully, you will never need to draw it."

"Where am I going, and who with?"

"You are to lead the children out of the city and away from here where they will be safe, over the mountains following the goatherd's path, to the land of the Kusai. You must travel only during the hours of darkness so that you will not be seen until you are out of sight of the city and the Plain of Trion."

"And you and mother," he said, breathlessly, his voice rising, "are you not coming? What is to happen?"

"We must stay here," said Tormon, "and defend the inner citadel until you have crossed the mountains. Then…" he hesitated, "then we will follow."

"You won't be able to," said Zeth. "It's impossible for you to take everyone out of the city without being seen. I will not go; I will stay here and fight and die with you. I will not leave you. Let the children go with someone else – let them go with Zia."

Tormon put his arm around his son in a rare show of affection. "My son," he said, "this is how it must be. It is not for us to choose now. We all must take a hard, hard road because there are no easy roads left. Every child that has been told they must go feels like you tonight, and the only child they will follow now is you. You can give them just enough courage to take those first steps to their safety across a bridge of lies that has been built for them by their parents. And you know what I mean, don't you?"

"But," replied Zeth, "I don't feel I can go now. I would prefer to die here with you; I can't move myself to go."

"We knew it would be like this," said Lelka. "Did you think we don't know you? So, we have contrived this to turn your heart, just enough." She opened the gates to the courtyard that opened onto the street and there, standing as far as the eye could see, were all the children of Trion, forlorn, sad and waiting, waiting for Zeth. Leading them was Zia with her knowing, rebellious smile.

"We all must do what we need to do now, Zeth. They are waiting for you and everyone in Trion needs you now to lead them out of here and save the best of Trion for us. Zia has been told everything – what you must do, where you must go."

Zeth looked at the sea of frightened faces and knew then that he had to go; he could not refuse. He threw himself into his mother's arms and his father embraced them both. "Please, please," he begged, "try to come, try to escape and join us!"

"We will try," said Tormon. "We will try."

Chapter Fifteen

Yan's Last Charge

Yan stood by the main gate, holding the reins of Dava's horse. He patted the horse's neck and breathed in deeply the cold evening air. "One last ride for you and me, my friend," he said. "You saved me once – will you do it again?"

His instructions were clear: to lead the last charge out of Trion and distract Agon's troops whilst the children escaped. He was to wait until the last of the sun's rays disappeared below the horizon and then lead his one hundred and five riders out of the city and across the plain to Agon's camp.

The debris between the gates had already been cleared and soldiers were waiting to turn the great gearing mechanism that would haul the treadled drawbridge across the ditch for the horses to cross. Each rider held a spear with its shaft wrapped in flammable oil ready to be lit.

The instructions from Tormon were clear: "Ride to the edge of Agon's camp and throw your spears into anything that will burn, then turn and ride back as swiftly as possible. With any luck, you will all return alive – we want no heroes.

We will need all of you back to help with the last defence of the city. Your spears will do the work, spreading fire and confusion within Agon's camp. With any luck, even his scouts roaming the plain will hurry back when they see the fires, leaving the path clear for the children."

Yan looked up at the watchtower. He could just make out the figure of Tormon, who was stood, waiting for the sun to set, holding his lighted torch below the parapet, ready to give the signal to open the gates. The figure suddenly turned completely black, then disappeared – he could see nothing. Then, there it was, two waves of the burning torch. He could hear the great gates swinging open. He took a deep breath and swung himself up into the saddle and started to move towards the gates, his troop following him slowly.

As they trotted over the drawbridge, a file of soldiers with torches lit their spears. It felt like a festival, the bright yellow and red flames dancing merrily against the black night sky, the horses' breath caught in the light of the flames. As they exited the gate onto the plain, they spread out into a long line with Yan in front at the centre. They were well instructed – they set off at a slow canter behind Yan. Then Yan picked up the pace a little and they followed. Then again, and again until they were galloping at full speed as they approached Agon's camp, with its ramshackle defences of wooden barricades, carts and tree trunks blocking their way.

Yan threw his spear high into the air, aimed at a large tent behind the barricades. The other riders followed suit in unison, sending a rain of fire into Agon's camp. Fires sprang up wherever the spears landed – in tents, along the barricade and in siege engines prepared for the next assault upon the city – causing chaos within the camp.

The riders, as instructed, swung round and raced back towards the city before the Lion-men could respond. All, that is, except Yan who, exhilarated by the charge, could not help himself. He dug his spurs into his horse and jumped the barricade, drawing his sword as he did so. He sliced through a Lion-man as he strove to run out of his path, then slashed the throat of another who ran forward to challenge him. He galloped through the Agon's camp, cutting tie ropes with his sword, sending tents flopping to the ground and felling every Lion-man he could reach in his path. Then he swept back towards the city to make his escape, jumping the barricade once more, exultant, happy. But he had scarce time to pick up pace when he felt the thud of an arrow in his back. He jerked forward, resting his head upon the horse's neck. He knew instantly that he would not make it. Sensation drained from his body before he felt any pain. The horse kept running for a while but then, feeling no impulse from its rider, slowed to a confused, slow canter halfway to the gates.

Yan felt the life drain from his body, feeling no more fear, only a weariness and a kind of relief as he slipped from the horse to the ground.

Chapter Sixteen

Without the City Walls

Dusk: Zeth and Zia climbed a little up the hill, away from the children who were scattered all along the edge of the forest they had just passed through. They wanted a last look at Trion before the sun set. They had walked through most of the night, as they had been instructed, until at last, the younger children, bewildered and exhausted, could walk no more, and they stopped and allowed them to sleep in the forest through to the end of the night and on into the late morning.

Somehow, they had managed to keep the children occupied in the forest through the afternoon until dusk, eating their first day's rations, telling them stories, allowing them to huddle in groups of friends and talk anxiously to each other. But it had not been easy – some wanted to go back; they could not understand what was happening. Now it was time to push on into the foothills of the mountains, but first this last look to see if they could make out what was happening.

There it was, in the fading light, the city that had been their home for all their lives. There was no sign of activity around the walls, but beyond them there was an orange glow and smoke. There could be no doubt – there was fire inside the city. Zeth was dimly aware of a tear trickling down his face.

"They're not coming, are they?" said Zia. "They never were, were they? They are going to hold out, as long as they can, so that we can escape. That was always the plan, wasn't it?"

Zeth nodded his head. There was no point in lying, not to Zia.

"It's heroic, isn't it?" she said. "Like in the stories."

"Yes," replied Zeth. "It's heroic, just like in the stories."

A voice broke their thoughts – it was Hela, a girl from the band they had been in during the last harvest, so long ago now. She was tending to the grazed knee of a young boy and reassuring him as she cleaned and covered the graze with a salve, using the skills she had been taught in the House of Healing.

Did it matter, one grazed knee and one act of kindness amid all this destruction and loss of life? *Yes*, thought Zeth, *it mattered as much as anything*. His visionary eye was suddenly filled with the wonder of it; it was an act that filled immensity. It was almost as though he was back in Trion, before all this had happened. He realised that this was what was normal: kindness and sympathy. Agon was an aberration, a monster – in the end, it would be the many acts of kindness that one day would defeat him. It was only a matter of time. Even this one act was a spear in the side of Agon and all like him. He saw that kindness, too, was an act of the imagination, as important as any image. And he saw, remembering Iordic, that kindness and compassion was not limited to the people of Trion but was common to all people – it was what it meant to be human.

He drew a deep breath and said, "Come on, Zia, we have to go; we have to go and build a better city." Zia looked at him, startled by his sudden change of mood. She put her arm around his shoulders – the first time she had done such a thing – and said, "They were right when they chose you to lead us, Zeth – you always find hope, don't you? You always haul yourself up from the depths of despair and find something to live for! But tell me, how are you going to get these exhausted children to take another step towards the mountains?"

As she spoke, they were startled by the noise of rushing air above them. All the children turned towards it, looking up. A great, golden eagle landed on a rock behind Zeth and Zia. Its wings caught the dying light of the sun and gleamed, brilliantly. The children gaped, awestruck. Then, as it took to the air again, they all leapt to their feet, fearful it might attack. It hovered over them for a moment, gazed down upon them with an air of arrogant unconcern, then turned, and with one beat of its wings, it flew, upwards towards the mountains.

The children, without thinking, moved after it and took their first step, following Zeth, the image-maker, who was already striding away, over the mountains, to build a new city, a city without walls.